Y0-BYZ-917

Savannah Spectator Blind Item

Q: What does a runaway heiress from the Wild West do while she's hiding from her powerful family?

A: Assume the identity of a plain-Jane executive assistant to one of Savannah's richest and sexiest bachelors!

But rumor has it she's doing more than typing memos for the boss, if you get our drift. One look at the much younger woman, and Mr. Boss was planning his Barry White play list and rewriting the company's "no fraternizing" rule book. But if this is love, then what will our heiress do when her family comes to "rescue" her from the Big Bad Boss?

The Savannah Spectator says this: two fortunes are better than one, so anticipate a society wedding the size of the entire state of Georgia!

Dear Reader,

We're so glad you've chosen Silhouette Desire because we have a *lot* of wonderful—and sexy!—stories for you. The month starts to heat up with *The Boss Man's Fortune* by Kathryn Jensen. This fabulous boss/secretary novel is part of our ongoing continuity, DYNASTIES: THE DANFORTHS, and also reintroduces characters from another well-known family: The Fortunes. Things continue to simmer with Peggy Moreland's *The Last Good Man in Texas,* a fabulous continuation of her series THE TANNERS OF TEXAS.

More steamy stuff is heading your way with *Shut Up And Kiss Me* by Sara Orwig, as she starts off a new series, STALLION PASS: TEXAS KNIGHTS. (Watch for the series to continue next month in Silhouette Intimate Moments.) The always-compelling Laura Wright is back with a hot-blooded Native American hero in *Redwolf's Woman. Storm of Seduction* by Cindy Gerard will surely fire up your hormones with an alpha male hero out of your wildest fantasies. And Margaret Allison makes her Silhouette Desire debut with *At Any Price,* a book about sweet revenge that is almost too hot to handle!

And, as summer approaches, we'll have more scorching love stories for you—guaranteed to satisfy your every Silhouette Desire!

Happy reading,

Melissa Jeglinski

Melissa Jeglinski
Senior Editor, Silhouette Desire

Please address questions and book requests to:
Silhouette Reader Service
U.S.: 3010 Walden Ave., P.O. Box 1325, Buffalo, NY 14269
Canadian: P.O. Box 609, Fort Erie, Ont. L2A 5X3

DYNASTIES: THE DANFORTHS

THE BOSS MAN'S FORTUNE

KATHRYN JENSEN

Published by Silhouette Books

America's Publisher of Contemporary Romance

If you purchased this book without a cover you should be aware
that this book is stolen property. It was reported as "unsold and
destroyed" to the publisher, and neither the author nor the
publisher has received any payment for this "stripped book."

Special thanks and acknowledgment are given to
Kathryn Jensen for her contribution to the
DYNASTIES: THE DANFORTHS series.

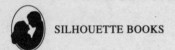 **SILHOUETTE BOOKS**

ISBN 0-373-76579-7

THE BOSS MAN'S FORTUNE

Copyright © 2004 by Harlequin books S.A.

All rights reserved. Except for use in any review, the reproduction
or utilization of this work in whole or in part in any form by any
electronic, mechanical or other means, now known or hereafter
invented, including xerography, photocopying and recording, or in
any information storage or retrieval system, is forbidden without
the written permission of the publisher Harlequin Enterprises Limited,
233 Broadway, New York, NY 10279 U.S.A.

All characters in this book have no existence outside the imagination of
the author and have no relation whatsoever to anyone bearing the same
name or names. They are not even distantly inspired by any individual
known or unknown to the author, and all incidents are pure invention.

This edition published by arrangement with Harlequin Books S.A.

® and TM are trademarks of Harlequin Books S.A., used under license.
Trademarks indicated with ® are registered in the United States Patent
and Trademark Office, the Canadian Trade Marks Office and in other
countries.

Visit Silhouette Books at www.eHarlequin.com

Printed in U.S.A.

Books by Kathryn Jensen

Silhouette Desire

I Married a Prince #1115
The Earl Takes a Bride #1282
Mail-Order Cinderella #1318
The Earl's Secret #1343
The American Earl #1347
The Secret Prince #1428
The Royal & the Runaway Bride #1448
Mail-Order Prince in Her Bed #1498
The Boss Man's Fortune #1579

Silhouette Intimate Moments

Time and Again #685
Angel's Child #758
The Twelve-Month Marriage #797

KATHRYN JENSEN

has written over forty novels for adults and children,
under various names, and lived in many interesting
places, including Texas, Connecticut and Italy. She cur-
rently resides in Maryland with her husband and two
feline writing companions, Miranda and Tempest, who
behave precisely as their names indicate—the first,
sweetly…the second, mischievously. Their thirty-two-
foot sailboat, *Purr,* promises to carry all four on many
new adventures. Aboard her is where Kathryn does
much of her summer writing.

DYNASTIES: THE DANFORTHS

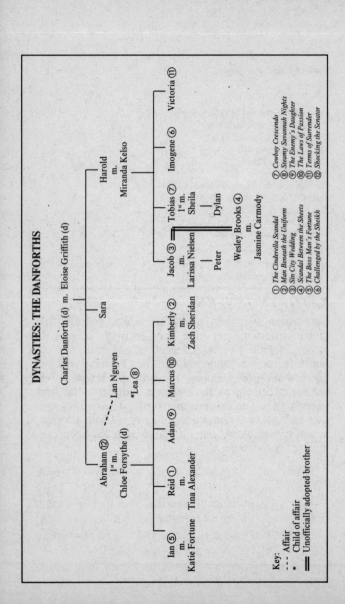

Charles Danforth (d) m. Eloise Griffith (d)

Abraham ⑫ 1st m. Chloe Forsythe (d) — Lan Nguyen

Sara

Harold m. Miranda Kelso

*Lea ⑧

Reid ① m. Tina Alexander

Ian ⑤ m. Katie Fortune

Adam ⑨

Marcus ⑩

Kimberly ② m. Zach Sheridan

Jacob ③ m. Larissa Nielsen

Tobias ⑦ 1st m. Sheila

Imogene ⑥

Victoria ⑪

Peter

Dylan

Wesley Brooks ④ m. Jasmine Carmody

① The Cinderella Scandal
② Man Beneath the Uniform
③ Sin City Wedding
④ Scandal Between the Sheets
⑤ The Boss Man's Fortune
⑥ Challenged by the Sheikh
⑦ Cowboy Crescendo
⑧ Steamy Savannah Nights
⑨ The Enemy's Daughter
⑩ The Laws of Passion
⑪ Terms of Surrender
⑫ Shocking the Senator

Key:
- - - Affair
* Child of affair
═══ Unofficially adopted brother

One

"**I**'ve found her, sir!" The cheerful voice coming from Ian Danforth's cell phone delivered the first good news he'd heard in weeks.

His early-morning workout interrupted, the young CEO of Danforth & Danforth Import Company reached for his towel on the exercise bench in the executive gym. He pressed it to his sweat-beaded forehead, then draped the plush white swath of Egyptian cotton around his damp shoulders.

"Excellent," he panted, trying to catch his breath. "When can she start?"

"She's from the temp service, able to begin right away." Holly Francis, his personnel manager, sounded relieved. "Her name is Katie O'Brien. I've spoken with her, and I think you'll like her. She's a very self-assured young woman, seems to have good people skills, although not a great deal of office—"

"I don't require a biography of the woman," Ian interrupted impatiently.

He rolled one shoulder then the other to ease muscles knotted by three sets of hundred-pound bench presses. Ease up, Danforth, he scolded himself. It wasn't poor Holly's fault that his executive assistant had left so suddenly. Neither was she to blame for the reason he was wound so tight. His family's problems had become serious issues for the company.

It had all started with his father, Abraham Danforth's, bid for the U.S. Senate. Then one crisis after another had struck the distinguished Georgia family and their successful import company. The final straw had been recently losing his executive assistant. But none of that made snapping at poor Holly acceptable.

He tried to mellow his tone. "She's just a temp. As long as she can answer a phone and file, she'll do until you find me a permanent replacement."

"Of course, sir." There was only the slightest hesitation before Holly came back at him with exaggerated sweetness. "And shall I send this young woman directly into the lion's den or—"

"That will be enough, Miss Francis." But Ian couldn't help smiling. Thank God, someone around there was holding on to a sense of humor during all the recent turmoil.

The body of a young woman had been found in his parents' attic, and the discovery had shocked the entire family. The young woman had turned out to be the housekeeper's disturbed daughter who had died of a longtime condition. Then, an unexplained explosion in this very building, and pressure coming from suspicious sources in Colombia to switch suppliers for

D&D's imported coffee beans had all but tapped his good humor.

He thanked the powers-that-be the five-story, antebellum-style Savannah headquarters had been empty when the bomb went off. No one had been injured. Still, extensive damage had been done to one floor. Both the family and the police were taking the incident seriously.

And, as CEO, Ian felt responsible for his employees' safety. The police hadn't yet been able to establish who had planted the explosives, but it was clearly a professional job, meant to intimidate—aimed at forcing Ian and his family to move in a direction he refused to take. He shook off the dark thoughts, telling himself to face the day one simple step at a time.

"I'll get changed and meet her on the fifth floor."

"She's on her way over. I'll escort her up to your office myself."

"Thanks, Holly. I do appreciate your efforts, really." He clicked off the cell and headed for the shower.

Losing his executive assistant without warning had made last week hell. He had depended on Gloria since his father had handed over the reins of the company to him, his eldest son. But not because he was too old to continue leading his family's multimillion-dollar import business. Abraham, the tough-as-steel Vietnam veteran, thrived on challenges and was a natural leader. So it seemed inevitable he would seek public office at some point in his life. Having hit his fifties, the time seemed right.

Honest Abe II—that's what his campaign manager had dubbed him, making the most of his squeaky-clean image. Now it was critical to keep him above reproach by resolving possible sources of scandal, quickly and without exposure to the press.

But in the meantime, Ian needed to keep the company moving forward. In addition to overseeing the import side of the corporation, Ian also directed a national chain of gourmet coffee shops, D&D's, that he himself had established as an offshoot of his father's and grandfather's original company.

Gloria had been a gem. She'd made sure he remembered critical meetings and ran interference by screening nuisance calls and fending off the press when things had started heating up for the family. But her mother had suddenly taken ill, and she'd understandably needed to go to her. Last he'd heard, she was moving back home to Ohio to care for her. He made a mental note to have Holly track down the address. He'd send flowers.

Twenty minutes later, Ian had changed into a tropical-weight, taupe Armani suit and stepped off the elevator on the fifth floor. He grunted a good-morning to several employees bustling along the corridor and pushed through the heavy oak door to the CEO's office suite.

A young woman with a wealth of curly auburn hair looked up at him from the reception-area couch where she sat primly, an expectant gleam in her green eyes. She looked terribly young compared to Gloria. Shooting to her feet the moment she saw him, she stepped eagerly forward and stuck out her hand.

"Mr. Danforth, I'm so very glad to be working for you," she said breathlessly. "You can't imagine how excited I am to be here, in a real office, doing...doing important things. If there's anything at all you want me to do, just say so. Maybe the temp agency told you that I haven't had a lot of experience…'' The words tumbled out of her, one on top of another, so that he had trouble untangling them. ''But I learn really fast, and I'll work very, very hard. I swear you won't be disappointed.…''

He winced as she pumped his hand. He felt exhausted just listening to her.

''Stop!'' he barked.

She blinked up at him, and he caught his breath at the flash of those jade eyes. He felt as if they were pinning him to the carpet. ''Did I say something wrong?'' she asked.

Releasing her fingers from around his, he backed away from her and turned to open the door to his inner office. ''You talk too much.''

''I beg your pardon?'' She followed him into his office and across the dark blue Aubusson carpet toward his desk.

He waved her to a chair. ''Don't get too comfortable here, Miss O'Brien. Danforth and Company promotes from within whenever possible. We feel a certain loyalty to our employees.''

She smiled. ''That's commendable.''

He smiled back. ''Yes…well, Personnel has started interviewing candidates for this position. I doubt you'll be needed for more than a week or two, so just relax, answer the phone when it rings, keep the files in order, and you'll do just fine for your short visit with us.''

''Oh,'' she murmured, eyes downcast.

He felt a little sorry for her. But it wouldn't have been right to mislead her. ''Nevertheless, your brief presence here is important. Think of yourself as holding down the fort until the cavalry arrives.''

She immediately brightened. ''I can do that.''

He bet she could. With her youthful exuberance, she could probably stop a runaway train.

So what, he thought with a mental shrug. He liked her energy, although she made him a little dizzy. Sort of the way he felt if he put too much weight on the bar. Challenges were sometimes a good thing.

Walking around the back side of his desk, he mused over her accent. Definitely not native Georgian. Most likely not even Southern of any brand. Possibly Midwest?

It didn't really matter, he told himself. Temps came and went faster than a Savannah sunset.

"Have a seat," he said, halfway between an order and an invitation.

She sat.

"Do you type, Miss O'Brien?"

She looked across the desk at him, hesitating for a heartbeat, as if she wasn't sure he'd been speaking to her. "Oh, yes." She let out a nervous laugh. "Of course I type."

"Word-processing skills?"

"The usual." She smiled, sitting very straight, knees tucked together, hands folded demurely over them. Her slim calves were pressed together, as if she'd been told all of her life to "sit like a lady."

Something about her, he thought, didn't fit the picture. "What's your educational background, Miss O'Brien?"

"Katie," she said. "I want to be called Katie."

He pressed his shoulders into the high leather back of his chair, hands laced behind his head, and observed the perky redhead over an expanse of cool, dark mahogany. "All right, Katie, where did you go to school?"

The question seemed to require some thought before she could answer. "Belmont College." She nodded, as if the words sounded right to her.

"I don't believe I've heard of it."

"It's a small college in Arizona. Sort of—" green eyes flickered, making his heart jump "—a community college."

"I see. Have you ever worked in an office?"

She worried her bottom lip between small, very white, very straight teeth and observed him apprehensively. "No." She rushed on, "But like I said, I'm sure I can catch on fast enough. I type pretty fast. I'm a very good speller, and I like filing and—"

"You *like* filing?" He couldn't help chuckling.

Her eyes crackled, green fire. "Is there something amusing about honest hard work?"

"Not at all." He forced the curve out of his lips. Where, he wondered, was this sudden antagonism coming from?

"I can work just as hard and just as long as anyone else. All I'm asking for is a chance. If you're not going to give me that—" She shot to her feet, and he had a vision of her coming over the desk at him in a wave of female fury. Instead, she reached for her purse and spun toward the door. "I guess this interview was a waste of both your and my time."

"Wait!" he shouted.

For a moment, the room reverberated with the commanding sound of his voice.

Then, slowly, she turned to observe him with cool composure over one shoulder, a single eyebrow peaked, as if to say, *You dare raise your voice to me?* Just like that, the ingenue was gone. Like champagne bubbles evaporating into the air.

This young woman, he could now see, had a mind of her own. And spirit. Good, he thought. All the more interesting to work with.

He stood up behind his desk. "I'm sorry if I offended you, Miss O'Brien…Katie. Please stay."

Returning slowly to the center of the carpet, she watched him cautiously from beneath a thick fringe of lashes shades darker than her russet hair. "It's not as if I don't have other opportunities," she said. "I can be anything I want."

He studied her, intrigued by her choice of words. *Be* anything she wanted? Not *do*. He decided it would be safer not to ask. Unleashing her conversational talents again would be unwise.

"All I'm asking is that you help me keep my working days in order until we properly fill the position." He gestured toward the chair she'd vacated, and she returned to it. "This includes answering the telephone, responding to my e-mail, keeping my calendar straight, and accompanying me to a few meetings for the purpose of taking notes. Do you think you can do that?"

She nodded, her eyes wide, lips pressed in a solemn line, as if it took immense concentration for her to keep them from moving while he spoke. "Absolutely," she murmured.

"Good." He let out a long breath of relief, feeling as if he'd fought a damn war. And here it wasn't yet nine in the morning! "You may start tomorrow morning, if that's all right with you."

"Not today?" She looked disappointed.

"I have family business to take care of today. It wouldn't be fair to leave you all day on your own. But, if you like, take a look in Gloria's desk. She left detailed instructions and office procedures for her replacement. You might want to take those home to study. Tomorrow, at eight a.m. sharp, you can start filing while you cover the phone.''

''Great!'' Katie chirped. She flashed him a dazzling smile. For some reason, that worried more than reassured him.

''Katie O'Brien,'' she murmured to herself as she snuggled into the corner of the couch, with a cup of coffee and the folder she'd brought back to the apartment with her. *Goodbye, Katherine Fortune…hello, Katie O'Brien, her new persona.* ''Just you remember who you are,'' she warned herself, toasting this important day with the chipped coffee mug.

It was a little after lunchtime, and she'd only just returned from doing errands before settling in with what she considered her homework. Paid homework, she reminded herself cheerfully. Danforth was paying her even for this day of preparation.

Things were definitely looking up!

Leaving home had been impulsive, she admitted to herself. And more than a little frightening. That first day, as she'd hitchhiked to Tucson, she hadn't even considered a final destination. Then she realized she couldn't remain in Arizona without her family tracking her down and forcing her to come back to them.

Besides finding a safe place to start her new life as an independent woman, she had other worries. Not the least of which was supporting herself—something she'd never had to do before. She couldn't use her dad's credit cards or write checks off her bank account. Any purchases from family accounts could be traced. What she had to do was make a totally fresh start.

She'd paid cash for her bus ticket.

As the Greyhound had rolled east out of Arizona, she thought about one of her sorority sisters, Kate O'Brien. Just last month Kate had e-mailed her from Savannah, overjoyed with a new job that required her to live in Europe on an extended basis.

Kate had a reputation on campus for her crazy pranks, but Katherine had always admired her individuality and daring. And some of her ideas were actually pretty good! Katherine called her in London.

"If you really want to disappear," Kate suggested excitedly, "why not become me?"

"*Become* you?" Katherine had only hoped for a lead on a place to crash temporarily, until she could afford an apartment of her own, perhaps in Savannah.

"Sure. Everyone always said we look enough alike to be sisters. Twins, if it weren't for my red hair. I left my U.S. driver's license and other ID I knew I wouldn't need in my top bureau drawer at the condo. Since I just bought it a few months ago, I wasn't about to sell it. I didn't even get a chance to meet my neighbors before I got this offer. So no one in the neighborhood really knows me."

"I should pay you rent or something," Katherine suggested, "once I get a job."

"No rush. Just don't get any speeding tickets or commit a felony. You can be me as long as I'm gone. I don't know myself how long that will be."

And so, Katherine Fortune, heiress to a multibillion-dollar construction empire, had dyed her dark brown hair a sultry auburn, added a perm to duplicate her friend's lush curls, bought a pair of metal-rimmed eyeglasses with clear lenses at a drugstore…and become Katie O'Brien. It had been so easy she couldn't quite believe it even now.

The only difficult thing had been finding a job. Half the places she interviewed told her she was overqualified, just by virtue of having a college degree. Waitressing positions wanted "experienced only," and retail sales jobs were looking for particular backgrounds, too.

How was she supposed to get experience if everyone always wanted you to be experienced before they hired you? It was so frustrating.

Then the manager at one of the mall stores suggested she try a temp agency. "They're always short on reliable clerical help and may even train you some."

Katherine headed straight for Execu-Temps, and they just happened to have received an emergency call from a local coffee-import company.

Perfect! she thought. After all, she adored cappuccino. What more did she need to know?

Katie, she reminded herself again. She liked that far better than being called Katherine, which sounded so stuffy. And it was a legitimate nickname anyway. Maybe she'd keep it even after she got her life sorted out. She wouldn't have to hide from her family forever. Just long enough to discover what she wanted to do with her life and make a good start.

What *she* wanted to do, not what they expected her to do. She had an honest-to-goodness, real job. And she'd gotten it all by herself. Lord, it felt good!

And it would feel even better when she held her first paycheck. The temp agency promised it at the end of the week.

Meanwhile, she had enough food in the fridge, enough cash for crosstown bus fare if she needed it. The Danforth Building was actually close enough for her to walk to the office. Maybe she should stick to her feet and save what little she had in her purse for an emergency.

There would be no dinners at fancy restaurants, she told herself sternly, sipping her instant coffee laced with powdered creamer and pink sweetener. No shopping in those posh boutiques she'd glimpsed while strolling down Broughton Street. No manicures, pedicures, massages or any of the little luxuries she'd grown up enjoying…until she could afford to pay for them with her own money.

A simple life…her own decisions…her own friends, which she was sure she'd soon make. This was *her* life. Her parents and uncles and their financial advisors would soon realize that. She'd prove to them all that she could fend for herself. They could take their plans for turning her into another spoiled society wife and—

Katherine-now-Katie caught her breath at the sharp jangle of the telephone. Her heart hammering in her chest, she ran the tip of her tongue between lips that suddenly felt as parched as if she were standing under a desert sun back home.

What if she picked up the phone and it was her father or one of her brothers? They would recognize her voice.

But they didn't know where she was. Or did they?

Drawing a deep breath, she waited. Three rings… four rings…five… By the sixth, she couldn't take it any longer and cautiously lifted the receiver.

"Hello?"

"Miss Katie O'Brien, please," a deep voice intoned.

Warmth rippled through her, restoring sensation to numb fingertips and toes at the thought of the handsome executive who had interviewed her earlier that day. His dark hazel eyes and striking face instantly came to mind.

"Yes, this is Katie," she answered in a breathless whoosh.

"Ian Danforth here. I forgot to inform the temp agency that you'd need to be on call weekends, as well as during the week. Is that a problem for you?"

"I, well, I don't think so," she said, although it seemed a little odd to be expected to work seven days a week. Was that legal?

Maybe Danforth was the kind of boss who would take advantage of her inexperience. She had hoped for some time to herself. Once she'd saved up a bit, she wanted to explore the local clubs, fun places where people in their twenties hung out when they weren't working.

"That is," Katie added, "the agency said this was a minimum-wage position, and no one said anything about overtime pay."

"Don't worry," Danforth said, "we compensate our employees more than fairly."

But wasn't she, at least technically, an employee of the temp agency? Not a company employee.

She decided to let it go. After all, this was her first job. She didn't want to make waves. If she did well in the week or two she'd be with the coffee magnate, she might then be able to find a permanent position with an even larger firm. That would be even better, because the more anonymous she remained, the harder it would be for her family to track her down.

"All right," she said. "If I'm really needed on weekends, I can be available."

"Good."

When he said nothing more, she asked, "Is there anything else, Mr. Danforth?"

"Ian," he said. "If you're going to insist upon me calling you Katie, then I'm Ian."

"Fine," she said, considering the motives behind this last request.

She wasn't normally suspicious of people, but she'd been around powerful men all of her life. As a Fortune woman, she'd learned to be wary when one of those men chose to cross the line between business and pleasure.

She wasn't looking for romantic entanglements with any man whose authority or personal wealth came close to her own family's.

"Then I'll see you tomorrow morning at eight." She made her voice as crisp and appropriately businesslike as possible.

"Yes, of course." Ian sounded unsure, and she wondered if she'd come off just a little too imperious. She could almost hear an echo of her grandmother's tone when reprimanding a servant. Katie grimaced and held her breath. Maybe he'd guess she wasn't who she claimed?

"Nine will be early enough," he said at last. "Be ready for a long day. There's a lot to be done." The line clicked, the dial tone returned.

Still suspicious, Katie stared at the phone in her hand. She might be new to the working world, but she'd dropped in on her father's office enough to know that CEOs of high-profile companies didn't call temps to clarify working hours. They had staff to see to such mundane details.

So, why had Ian Danforth called her?

Katie sighed, all the triumph of the day fading away

to worry. She'd have to be extremely careful not to blow her cover. She desperately wanted to do well, to be on her own and away from the smothering influence of her family. Away from her mother who so desperately begged her to consider marriage, although she was only twenty-two.

Already, more than one suitor had approached Tyler Fortune, asking permission to court his daughter. But she wasn't in love with any of them, and she wasn't going to marry for less than love.

Katie hung up the phone and opened the refrigerator door to study its contents. Eggs, milk, cheese, a cellophane bag of mixed greens. This would do for a very nice omelette and salad. She'd eat in—thereby saving money—and study the office file, maybe watch TV for an hour or so, then turn in early. She wasn't used to rising before nine in the morning, but she'd need to be up at seven if she was to have time to shower, do her hair, dress and be at her new job on time.

Katie smiled. It wasn't going to be easy. Not any of it. But it was an adventure. *Her* adventure! And she'd darn well make the most of it.

Two

"This isn't an amusement park, Miss O'Brien."

Katie dropped one foot to the floor and stopped the wheeled office chair from spinning. She'd arrived a little early but wasn't sure where to begin. The phone had been silent, and Danforth wasn't in his office.

But now Ian hung in the doorway like a thundercloud.

Katie stood up quickly, still a little dizzy. "Just testing the equipment," she said with as much decorum as she could muster.

"The chair works," he said dryly.

"Yes, it does…seem to." She looked down at it, trying to appear concerned about some mechanism that hadn't functioned quite to her satisfaction. "I think it will do."

"Are you ready to get to work?" he asked. Not a hint of a smile lifted his lips or lit his eyes.

"Yes." She cleared her throat. "Absolutely ready."

"Good." He pointed to the computer on her desk. "Please bring up my agenda for the day. I'll also need files pulled for the coffee-bean suppliers I'm scheduled to meet with in the next few weeks. And there's everything required to make coffee in that cabinet over there. I take mine black."

"Agenda," she repeated, nodding solemnly as he started through the door to his office, "files and coffee. Right away, sir."

This was going to be a snap. And a wonderful learning experience, she assured herself as she settled into her well-tested chair and flicked the toggle switch that turned on the computer.

The chair bit had been sort of childish, she admitted to herself, but fun. Life, even the working life, didn't have to be so very solemn and drab, did it?

She waited while the PC booted up. She'd had a laptop computer since she was a child, and used one all through college. But she'd had to leave it back in Arizona for lack of a way to carry it. She'd needed clothes more.

The desktop screen appeared on the monitor. Everything on it looked foreign to her.

She tried to access several files, but every one of them requested a password. She couldn't recall reading anything about that in the file she'd studied last night. Katie rummaged through several drawers but found nothing that would help her.

Her phone buzzed. Katie sat up straight and grinned at it. Her first official call! Her heart raced as she reached for the receiver.

"Danforth and Danforth, Ian Danforth's office," she announced formally.

"Are you planning on delivering my day's agenda sometime before the day is over, Miss O'Brien?"

Katie gritted her teeth and glared into the earpiece of the receiver. She counted very slowly to three. "I'm having a little trouble accessing the calendar. It will take me another minute or two." She hung up.

With a huff, she squinted at the screen. She typed a few letter/number sequences. No matter what she tried, angry amber words blinked at her: Access Denied.

"Under the blotter."

She looked up, startled.

Ian leaned against the doorjamb, his suit jacket off, white shirt cuffs rolled up to reveal muscular forearms. "Gloria left access information under her blotter. Not the most secure arrangement, but she wanted to make sure I wasn't locked out of the system."

Now that he mentioned it, she seemed to remember something about the blotter and a code. But there had been so much data in the file to absorb. And it was more than a little distracting, working in a private office with a man who looked like something off the cover of *GQ*.

Ian approached her desk. "Never mind, I need the time of my first appointment now." He reached over her shoulder for the keyboard.

"No, really, I'll do it," she insisted, trying to body-block him while prying up the corner of her blotter.

She pulled out a neatly typed three-by-five card, but he wheeled her chair aside with her in it. "Save that for later," he grumbled. "I'll bring up today's schedule. Apparently you'll need a good twenty-four hours to find it."

Katie saw fire.

Her rage wasn't of the puny match-flame sort. All of Savannah was ablaze.

Rocketing out of her chair, she squeezed herself between Ian and the computer, knocking his hand aside with the well-aimed thrust of one hip. "This is *my* job, and I'll do it!" She spun around to confront him.

He stepped back from their chest-to-chest face-off and scowled down at her. The man was a good two heads taller than she, outweighed her by at least eighty pounds of pure muscle, and his hazel eyes were menacingly dark.

She didn't care. She wasn't going to let Ian Danforth bully her any more than she was going to let her family push her around.

"Go back to your desk," she commanded. "I'll bring you a cup of coffee along with your day's appointments in ten minutes. Do you think you can wait that long?"

He looked more intrigued than angered by her nerve. Without a word, he meekly retreated into his office.

Katie let out the breath she'd been holding. What had possessed her to talk to the man that way? She was a temp; he could fire her on a whim! Then where would she be? The agency might refuse to place her again if she messed up her first assignment.

But she couldn't let him just walk all over her, now could she?

Coffee, she thought, flinging open cabinet doors and finding a drip-type coffeemaker. She'd promised the man coffee, and she could use a cup, too. She had been in such a rush to reach the office on time she hadn't eaten breakfast, although there was a nifty-looking coffee shop on the first floor. Evidently, Ian liked a steady supply close at hand, hence the in-office brewing station.

She found a stash of D&D's brand, premeasured gourmet-coffee filter bags. Soon a fresh, steaming pot was dripping away. It smelled heavenly, and she was tempted to pour herself a cup and gulp it down before taking Ian his. But she figured she shouldn't press her luck.

While the coffee finished up, she tapped out the keystrokes from the card and up popped his agenda for the day. She grinned, pleased with herself.

When she entered Ian's office minutes later, carrying a tray with a tall blue ceramic mug brimming with fragrant coffee, he was standing in front of a wide expanse of glass. Beyond the windows spread the elegant old city, glimpses of blue river showing between buildings both historic and modern.

"It's beautiful," she commented, setting the tray on his desk, then placing the neatly printed agenda beside it.

He turned to look at her. "Yes." A moment passed, and he seemed lost in thought. Then he was suddenly alert again. "My favorite time of year—the spring. What's it like where you come from, Katie?" The question was asked so casually that she didn't feel threatened.

"Hot. Arizona in May is already summer."

"You'll have trouble getting used to our humidity here," he said, moving back toward his desk. "Desert heat is much different from ours."

"Yes, I suppose. I have to get to that filing now," she said quickly. She could have lied, made up something about coming from another part of the country, but that sort of information was too easily checked.

She'd already decided to tell as much of the truth as possible, keep things simple.

"The filing can wait," he said, stopping her in her tracks. "Where's your cup?"

"I thought I'd wait until I'd given you your agenda and started the filing."

He glanced down at the sheet she'd given him. "We're going to be busy in here for quite a while. If you want any before lunch, you'd better get yourself a cup now."

Katie shrugged. "All right."

She found a second mug, pale green with magnolia blossoms, and poured herself some coffee. Before adding her usual sweetener and creamer, she sniffed the dark concoction. It was deliciously fragrant but she'd never drunk her coffee black. She loaded it up, snatched steno book and pen from her desk, and returned to his office.

Ian seemed intent upon papers on his desk and didn't look up at first. She sipped her coffee absently, opened the notebook to a clean page and awaited his instructions.

"You ruined it, didn't you?" he said, without looking up at her.

The cup stopped, suspended in front of her lips. "I what?"

"You doused D&D's best with chemicals. I can smell that god-awful stuff clear across the room."

"I like it this way," she said primly.

He shook his head in disapproval.

Katie straightened in her chair and took an unhurried sip. "Do your employees need your permission to choose what they eat and drink while at work?"

Ian placed his pen on the desk, laid both hands flat

over his paperwork and glared at her. "I was only trying to educate you, Miss O'Brien."

"Katie," she said demurely, and took another sip, all the more satisfying for the knowledge she was provoking him. "This really is pretty good coffee."

He looked as if he might be choking. "Pretty good?" he demanded, his face turning an interesting shade of red. "That's all you can say about my coffee?"

"Well, it is. Very rich, lots of body. I might have had better."

"I doubt that!" he roared. "We import only the very highest quality Colombian beans. And the roasting process is a secret known only to our plant managers."

"Really."

"Really. And if you stopped dumping garbage into your cup, you'd be able to tell the difference between excellent and pretty good."

Now that is quite enough, Katie thought. She put her cup down on the low glass table in front of her, laid her steno pad beside it and stood up.

Ian stared at her. "What?"

"I think I'll leave now."

"Where are you going?"

"Back to Execu-Temps to request a different assignment. The working conditions here are intolerable." She started for the door.

Before Katie could swing it all the way open, Ian had charged from his desk and dived in front of her. "What the hell does that mean?"

She gathered up her five-foot-four supply of feminine outrage and met his angry gaze head-on. "It means, Mr. Danforth, there's a clear line between reasonable requests from an employer and interfering with an employee's personal life.''

"I was just suggesting—"

"No, you weren't," she shot back at him, feeling heat rise up her cheeks. "You were dictating how I should drink my coffee. That isn't mentioned in the job requirements."

"Oh, for crying out loud," he muttered.

"It's not a little thing!" she insisted, getting more worked up by the moment.

But she was also aware of how close they were standing. And his fingers had somehow gotten wrapped around her arm when he tried to stop her from leaving the room. She tried to put his proximity out of mind. That only made her more aware of the size and heat of his body.

"Personal choices should be honored by other people," she stated.

"And the way you drink your coffee is one of these choices?"

"Yes." She gave him her best imitation of her grandmother, facing down one of her sons when she thought he'd stepped out of line.

Ian sighed and let his hand drop away from her. "Fair enough. But will you do me a favor?"

"What's that?" she asked, feeling a trifle meeker now that he had acquiesced to her point.

"If you're going to mess with D&D's coffee, at least do it with quality ingredients. Then tell me what you think of it."

She narrowed her eyes at him, but it seemed a compromise she could live with. "All right." Still, she shuddered to think what real sugar and cream would do to her figure if she got in the habit of using them all the time. "Just this once."

"Agreed."

She turned to retrieve her cup, but he beat her to it.

"Let me fix it for you. Then you can tell me how it compares with your usual cup of morning mud."

Arrogant, she thought. The man should have been born a couple centuries earlier...with a scepter in his hand. It was a wonder the woman she replaced had waited for a family emergency to jump ship.

Katie followed Ian back to the outer office. He took a small carton of cream from the minifridge beneath the coffeemaker, poured a dollop of rich, thick stuff into her cup, then added a single spoonful of sugar and stirred before topping off the cup with coffee.

"I take at least three sugars in coffee that strong," she said.

"You won't need them. This coffee is an espresso blend, from a naturally sweet bean. You kill the flavor by adding too much sugar."

The man was persistent, she'd say that much for him. But she would give him only her honest opinion, not empty praise just to satisfy his ego.

"Taste it as you would a good wine," he advised.

She took a sip and let the comfortably warm liquid settle over and around her tongue before it slipped down her throat. There was a silkiness to the coffee, a hint of spice and earth. A mist of aromatic steam rose to her face on the second sip, delighting her nostrils with a whiff of rain-forest nuttiness.

"Oh my," she whispered after swallowing again.

"What do you think now?" He waited, watching her expression intently. Her opinion, it seemed, mattered a great deal to him.

"It's...why, it's wonderful. I've never had better."
Although he couldn't possibly know it, her parents
kept only the very finest foods and beverages in their
home—much of it imported. Not until entering college
had she been exposed to grocery-store coffee. In all
ways, she'd truly been sheltered. "This is the product
you sell in D&D's coffee shops?"

"One of the blends, yes. It's my personal favorite."

"I can see why." She drank heartily from her mug,
holding it with both hands, never lowering it more than
a few inches from her face to better breathe in the
luscious aroma. "May I have another cup?" she asked
as she swallowed the last of it.

He looked pleased at her approval. "Certainly."

"It's all right. I'll fix it this time." She tossed him
a grin. "Don't worry. I won't kill it."

He watched as she carefully followed his lead for
the amount of cream then added half the sugar he had.
"Now," he said when she'd taken her first sip of the
fresh cupful, "I think we can get to work. That is, if
you're willing to stay and slave under the whip of a
dictator."

She felt herself blush at how close he'd come to the
image she'd had in mind. "I didn't call you that."

"No, you implied it. I'll try not to brandish my cat-
o'-nine-tails if you attempt not to overreact to an occasional request."

"Fair enough," she said, swallowing another
steamy mouthful.

Delicious. She wondered how many cups per day
would constitute an overdose.

Three

The moment Ian walked into the First City Club, he felt the knot at the back of his neck loosen. He hadn't realized how stressful the morning had been, breaking in his temp. Katie had a way of draining a man.

But it was hard to complain. She listened attentively, politely to every word he said but didn't miss a beat before correcting him if he slipped: asking for the wrong file, giving her a list of tasks when she felt his priorities should be different. Both her mind and body seemed to run on high-octane. Introducing her to good coffee, he suspected, had only aggravated the situation.

The woman was positively exhausting.

But now he was ensconced in one of his favorite places in the world. At the discreet Savannah members-only club, he was immediately recognized and greeted by the maître d', "Good day, Mr. Danforth." With crisp efficiency, Paul escorted him to his father's table, situated in a prime location at the window most distant from the kitchen.

Abraham Danforth and Nicola Granville, his campaign manager, were already seated, their heads lowered in conversation. Nicola tossed back her head and laughed, and Ian imagined the two of them sharing a joke at the expense of his father's opponent for the Senate, John van Gelder.

Then it came, the familiar sensation, like a belt cinching up around his chest. The painful sense of disappointment that he had so rarely succeeded in pleasing his own father, the man who had been absent throughout much of Ian's childhood. The man Ian respected and loved but who had always remained distant, if not cold.

Abraham had given his children so much in the way of material life, but so little love. As a man himself now, Ian understood how serving in the military on remote assignments and, later, losing a wife could harden a man. But the resentment he'd felt as a boy toward his father, for the precious little time they'd spent together, never really left.

It was his Uncle Harold and Aunt Miranda who had taken in Ian and his siblings during holidays away from boarding schools, who had given them all a sense of family and home. He looked at Abraham now, the veteran warrior. The tough gray-haired, steely-eyed entrepreneur, now engaged in another kind of battle.

Ian had no trouble envisioning his father, standing to speak before a joint session of Congress or sitting down to a cup of coffee with the president. The man was a born leader and would work hard to represent his beloved State of Georgia. So, despite the awkwardness that had always existed between them, Ian would support his father's bid for the Senate without reservation.

Nicola saw him coming first and smiled up at him as he took a seat across from them. "Great to see you again, Ian." She held out her hand across the pristine white linen, then tapped a polished nail on the menu. "I see Chef is serving your favorite—seared tuna."

The brief list of selections changed daily. And when reservations were made at the exclusive club by a member with particular tastes, Chef often added a dish or two to the day's selections.

"Great," Ian said as their waiter appeared to smoothly place Ian's napkin over his lap. "No need to even look at the menu."

Abraham greeted his son with a curt nod and his customary half smile. The man could be charming when he wanted to be, Ian had often noticed, but he wasted little warmth on family members. "Glad you could join us, Ian. We'll order then get down to business."

"Of course." Ian hid the hurt by turning toward the woman at his father's side. "Nicola, how's the campaign doing?"

"We've kicked into high gear, with aggressive advertising plans including television spots." Her eyes gleamed with excitement.

"Already? Isn't it a little early?"

She shook her head. "We have to jump right in, put a positive spin on your father's campaign. Too much recent press has been negative." She leaned across the table and continued with urgency. Her red hair, more orange than Katie's, seemed to flame up all the more brilliantly with her words. "Since we're billing him as

Honest Abe II, the man to be trusted, we can't afford any more questionable press."

"But nothing that's happened has been Dad's fault," Ian objected.

Abraham looked suddenly impatient. "No one at this table is debating that, Ian. Let's just have a look at the corporate figures you brought and see if there's anything we can do with those."

Ian felt as if someone had pulled the chair out from under him. He pressed his eyes closed for a second. "Damn. I can't believe I left the office without them."

The office.

The words conjured an image of Katie bouncing from her desk to the file cabinets to the coffee station for a refill. He shook off the instant sensation of warmth. "Sorry. I know you wanted to review those stats over lunch. I was thinking about other things. You see, I've got this temporary EA, and she's—"

"Good," Abraham snapped. "Give her a call. Tell her to bring the file down here right away. It'll take her ten minutes, tops."

"But I—" Ian didn't dare picture Katie in a place like this—a bastion of Savannah sophistication. This site of high-stakes corporate and political wheeling and dealing was no place for a nymph in department-store polyester.

"Is there a problem?" Abraham demanded.

"No, sir," Ian admitted reluctantly.

"Excellent. Give her a call."

With a sense of impending doom, Ian lifted his cell phone from its holster at his hip and punched the memory code for his office.

Nine minutes after she'd received Ian's call, Katie stepped out of a cab onto the busy Savannah street and glanced up at the impressive buildings around her. She'd been in Meccas of power similar to the First City Club. Feeding troughs for the elite, she thought of them.

This one, admittedly, seemed very appealing. The decor was sedate, tasteful, calming, she noticed as she whisked past a startled maître d'. He streaked after her, across the dining room.

"May we help you, miss?" Not a fraction of a smile for her in her plain black working-girl's skirt and white cotton blouse. His attitude stated that, clearly, she had entered the wrong door.

But Katie had dealt with all levels of snobbishness, had even dished out her own, she was embarrassed to admit, so she knew how to deal with it now.

Ratcheting her shoulders back and elevating her chin, she met his gaze with steel. "Mr. Danforth has requested I deliver this file to him."

The man reached for the leather folio into which she'd placed the file for protection. She hugged it to her chest. "Personally." She gave him an apologetic smile. "It's confidential."

The implication was subtle but nonetheless effective. She didn't expect he'd tamper with the file. But trust having been placed in her put her a step above him. It was just enough leverage to force the man to regard her as a professional and offer a show of respect.

"Certainly, miss. I will take you to the Danforth table at once."

He led the way through a room not unlike another she recalled in Tucson. She'd been there for a family meeting at which she'd been given very little say. The men in the family had done most of the talking. All the more reason for her to leave Arizona and seek her freedom elsewhere.

At the far end of the room, she could see Ian at a table with two other people. One of them, she assumed, was Ian's father. He sat straight backed, a harsh expression on his face. The lines of his jaw and squared-off shape of his shoulders resembled his son's. The woman seated to his left was considerably younger than the senior Danforth, very sharp in her business attire, and definitely attractive.

"Thank you, Miss O'Brien." Ian reached for the file even before she'd made it to the table.

She was aware of the maître d' shadowing her, as if to make sure she left the room without lingering. She ignored the man. The salads had been served and looked delicious. Her stomach grumbled.

"Do you need me for anything else while I'm here?" Katie asked. She felt Abraham studying her, glancing at Ian then back to her.

Ian quickly shook his head.

"I wonder if it might not be a good idea for Miss O'Brien to stay," suggested the older man. "It would be helpful to have notes on our meeting."

Ian looked worried. "I don't think that's necessary."

"I would appreciate it," Abraham said. He stood at the table, which meant Ian also had to stand or seem ungracious. "I'm Abraham Danforth, Ian's father, in case you hadn't guessed. And this is Nicola Granville, my campaign manager."

"Very pleased to meet you, sir," Katie said with a genuine smile. "And you also, Ms. Granville. I'd be pleased to stay if I can be of any help." She tossed

Ian a triumphant smirk, which he alone caught. She sat in the empty chair.

A waiter immediately shook out a napkin and draped it across her lap.

"Oh, I'm not eating," she objected, looking up at the man, who seemed confused.

"But you must," Nicola insisted, shifting her gaze to Abraham for confirmation. "Well, the poor girl is missing her lunch break for us, now isn't she?"

"Certainly," Abraham said, his smile unexpectedly disarming. The true politician, she thought. "I assume my son does allow you time to eat a meal now and then, Miss O'Brien?"

"Well, I've only been working for him since this morning, so I don't know—"

"Dad, let her order then we can start reviewing the file while we wait for our entrées."

"Do you have something to write on?" Nicola asked helpfully.

"I didn't expect to have to take notes, just deliver the file," Katie admitted. "But I'm sure that kind maître d' could supply writing materials."

"Never mind," Nicola said. She reached into her briefcase on the floor. "I've an extra pad, and pens galore. Will this do?" The slim, black pen had been printed in gold lettering with Abraham's campaign slogan: Honest Abe II for Senator!

"Perfect." Katie smiled at her.

Ian watched as Katie nibbled at a crusty roll and took notes. They covered not only the stats in the file but recent events that had wreaked havoc with the campaign and had impacted the entire family. Soon Katie was so engrossed in the details of their discussion she stopped eating as well as writing.

Ian had a very bad feeling about this. In the few hours he'd known Katie he'd learned one thing about her: the woman was hell on wheels when she started thinking.

"Did you get that last bit?" he asked, knowing she hadn't.

"Sorry." Katie picked up her forgotten pen, glanced at Abraham then back to Ian. "I find all of this just so amazing. Imagine discovering that poor woman's body in your attic! And a bomb going off in the very building where I'm working." She shook her head and *tsked* over the news. "And you really believe someone is stalking you, Senator?"

No one else objected to the premature title, so Ian let it go.

"We haven't exactly enjoyed a flawless beginning to the campaign," Nicola stated with a grim smile.

"I should say not," Katie agreed.

Ian tried to signal her to shut up before it was too late. She was walking on dangerous ground where his father was concerned. As genial as he'd been since Katie joined them, Abraham didn't take kindly to strangers interfering in the family's affairs.

But Katie barreled on, despite a subtle kick to her shin beneath the table. "The press must be having a field day with all of this."

Ian held his breath, expecting the worst. His father's temper was legend.

Abraham solemnly studied Katie for a long moment, then chuckled and shook his head. "You've hit that nail on the head, my dear. Unless we find a way to use these issues to our advantage, the press may well drive my campaign into the ground."

Katie sipped wine Abraham had ordered for the table. "Maybe it's already too late for that," she remarked thoughtfully. "Perhaps more drastic measures should be taken."

Ian moved her wineglass out of her reach. "Katie, you don't understand the complexity of—"

"No, let her explain herself," Abraham said, laying a hand on his son's arm. "Go ahead, my dear."

"Well, it seems to me that it's hard for people to take death lightly, unless there's an interesting ghost story behind it."

"Savannah has plenty of those," Nicola said.

"We even have a specter lurking around Crofthaven," Abraham remarked, referring to the family mansion.

"But not connected to the housekeeper's daughter," Ian pointed out.

"A tragedy," Nicola put in, "but not the murder the press initially assumed."

Katie nodded. "That's awful. But it still leaves you with a problem. If you can't make something go away or change it from bad news to good, then all you can do is distract people."

Abraham frowned. "Distract them? As in sleight of hand?"

Katie grinned and reached across the table in front of Ian to reclaim her wineglass. "Sort of."

Ian lost his appetite. Here goes, he thought.

"I mean," Katie continued, "give the press a better story to run with."

"She's right!" Nicola slapped the tabletop. "If a reporter stumbles onto something juicier, something that holds his attention long enough, he'll forget about old news and move on."

Abraham observed Katie through narrowed eyes. "Any specific ideas, young lady?"

Katie looked flustered for the first time since she'd entered the dining room. "I'd have to think about it. After all, I'm just here to take notes. Right?"

Good grief! Ian thought. One minute she was advisor to the family patriarch, the next she was the humble secretary. Did the woman have a split personality?

Nicola passed Katie one of those woman-to-woman smiles Ian detested, because they were almost always a portent of trouble. He tried to catch his father's eye to form up a male conspiracy of their own.

But Abraham was watching the two females with an amused smile. "You may have something there, Miss O'Brien," he said. "Thank you for your insight."

Ian rolled his eyes and gave up.

"That was some coup you pulled off at the club," Ian muttered as he steered through the historic district on their way back to Danforth & Danforth.

"What do you mean?" Katie asked nervously.

She had noticed Ian's irritation with her speaking out to his father and Ms. Granville. She hadn't meant to overstep the boundaries of her position, but it seemed impolite to refuse to stay when Abraham Danforth himself had requested her presence.

"I mean—" Ian made every syllable weighty "—I can count on one hand the people capable of charming my father and have fingers left over."

"Oh, please. I hardly—"

Ian let out a sharp laugh. "Don't pretend you didn't notice. You smiled, and the man melted faster than ice cream on a Georgia sidewalk in July."

She shrugged. "I just made a few suggestions, that's

all. Actually, I'd say it's Ms. Granville who has your dad's rapt attention.''

"Nicola?'' Ian huffed. "Of course he pays attention to her. She's his camp—''

"I know...I know, his campaign manager for the senatorial race.'' Katie turned on the leather passenger seat to face him as he drove. "But didn't you catch a...I don't know, an electric thing-y going on between them?''

"No.'' He was shocked at the very thought.

"Just a little?''

"Listen, Nicola's a pro. She wouldn't get romantically involved with a client. And my father, like many retired military officers, is obsessed with his next battle. This time it will be political, not military. But he won't waste his energy thinking about women. Believe me, I know.'' He failed to mask the bitterness in his voice. "Nothing distracts the man when he has his mind set on a goal.''

"Wouldn't be the first time politics and women ended up in the same bed.''

"You don't know what you're talking about,'' Ian grumbled. "Nicola and Dad...that's just insane.''

"If you say so.'' Katie turned to look out the tinted glass in the passenger window so Ian wouldn't see her smile.

It was so easy to get his goat, as her grandpa used to say. And so much fun. Almost as much fun as taunting her brothers when they were kids. At least now her prey wouldn't steal her dolls from her as punishment.

Katie cast a speculative glance at Ian in the driver's seat. He was a tall man, obviously strong. She guessed he must work out to keep in shape.

Her father had been an athlete in his youth; he'd told her about his days on college football fields. And he'd continued to lift weights even after he met her mother and they'd started having kids. Tyler Fortune had designed a fully equipped gym in the house he built for her mother on the edge of the desert, overlooking sacred Indian land where they'd fallen in love.

She vaguely remembered something about a legend, and a mystical cave where lovers became one in spirit. And, she guessed, in body as well. It had all sounded so romantic.

She wondered if Ian had a single romantic bone in his entire body. He was an appealing man with his wavy brown hair and shadowy eyes. His mouth was full, sensitive, and drew her eyes to his lips, as if something wonderful might come unexpectedly from them. Maybe words that would change her life in some mysterious way.

She felt suddenly light-headed and turned back to the window hurriedly.

"Well, it's a shame there isn't anything romantic going on between them. They'd make a handsome couple." She sighed.

"Never mind that. Your job was to record the meeting. As soon as we get back to the office, please type up your notes and give them to me. I want to take them home with me to think more about Dad's campaign in light of all that's been happening."

Katie tipped her head to observe him. "You really do look like him, you know."

For a moment she wondered if his silence meant he was angry with her. Then his expression softened. "You think so?"

"Mmm-hmm. Around the eyes. And your build. Some gestures, too."

He laughed. "Don't know how I picked up on those. Didn't seem he was around often enough while I was growing up for any of his habits to rub off."

"He traveled a lot with the military?"

Ian nodded. "And after. My uncle pretty much raised us kids. Good old Dad packed us all off to boarding school after my mother died. Holidays were nearly always spent with my uncle's family."

"I'm sorry," she murmured.

She couldn't imagine being without a close family. Without her mother, in particular. Yet here she was, intentionally separating herself from those she loved and who loved her. Strange, she thought, because she really did value them. But something deep inside her drove her to seek a life of her own.

"That must have been rough, being without your parents."

He shrugged, but his eyes had dimmed with pain. "All in the past now."

But is it, Ian? she thought.

"Besides, we had some great times—my brothers, sister and our cousins. To this day, when we all get together, we're like one big, loud family." He smiled, as if to demonstrate how okay he was with the past.

"Good," she said, deciding she would say nothing more on the topic. Let him keep that cheerful image. Even though she knew it was a poor substitute for the bond he'd sought but never found with his own father.

As soon as they were back in the office, Ian left Katie to type up her notes. He walked down two floors to Personnel. Holly looked up and smiled when he stepped through the open door to her office.

"Well, how's she working out, Ian?"

"Mixed reviews."

She looked surprised. "You don't like Katie? She seemed very personable, and smart, too."

"It's not that." He dug for a reasonable-sounding excuse. "I think she's overqualified for the job."

Holly leveled gray eyes at him. "A lot of college grads temp for a while, to feel their way into the work force."

"I know that." He raked fingers through his hair and paced in front of her desk. He couldn't explain the desperate need he felt to put space between himself and Katie. "Maybe it's just a personality clash. She doesn't act like...like an *employee*. She changes my requests and does things her own way. She even handed out advice to my father over lunch today!"

Holly laughed. "Wish I'd seen that."

He couldn't help the smile that teased his lips. "It was something to behold. What else do you know about her?"

"Aside from what's on the copy of the application I gave you?"

"Right." He propped both hands on her desk and leaned over the file she pulled in front of her from one corner of her desk.

Holly flipped pages. "Nothing of special interest. Graduated with a bachelor's degree in English. Worked a few summers for a construction company as a girl Friday, then as an occasional fill-in receptionist."

"Where?"

"Arizona, looks like." She scanned the form. "The temp agency might have more information on her."

"Nothing on her family? Where she grew up?"

She frowned up at him. "Why would you want to know that?"

"I don't know. It's just that something about her isn't right. It's been bothering me since yesterday. She doesn't act like a wet-behind-the-ears college grad from some hole-in-the-wall southwestern town. She's too poised, too sure of herself."

"You mean, you don't like that she doesn't jump when you say boo?"

Ian gave her a nasty look. "Do you have a sister, Holly? And is she sitting in my office at this very minute?"

She grinned. "Thank goodness you have a sense of humor or I would have lost my job long ago."

"Not a chance." He straightened up with a sigh. "You're too good at what you do for us to ever let you go."

She closed the folder on her desk and tapped it thoughtfully. "Tell you what, if you're really uncomfortable with Miss O'Brien, I'll step up our efforts to find you a permanent EA. That way, if we tell the temp agency her services are no longer needed, it won't reflect badly on her. We contracted to keep her for a month or less, dependent upon our filling the position."

"Good," he said. "The sooner she's out of here the better."

But even as he said those words, he doubted them.

Yes, she was annoying. Yes, she was difficult and made him restless in ways he couldn't understand. But she also challenged him, set him to thinking in new directions, with fresh energy.

Worst—or best—of all...she was damn good to look at. Maybe too good.

But all of that aside, there was something mysterious about Katie O'Brien. Something that deeply worried him even though he couldn't put his finger on what it was.

She would be trouble somewhere down the road, of that he was sure. She was a loose cannon aimed straight at his company and family. Her behavior at lunch today had proved at least that much. The Danforths had enough trouble without her making it worse.

Four

Cursing softly, Ian hung up the phone, hit the inter-office pager and pushed himself back from the polished ebony desk so large the delivery team had had to disassemble it to get it through his office door. He told himself to breathe. He focused on the smoky glass pane overlooking the Historic District pulsing with spring activity, willing away his black mood.

Delicate, creamy camellias and vivid crimson, pink, and lavender azaleas bloomed in profusion in a wash of Monet-like hues along the streets. Through the nearby park he could see Spanish moss lazily draping live oaks that had been around before he was born. Magnolia and sassafras trees reached gracefully for the sky. Traffic that roared and screeched in other cities merely hummed here. Cars were barred from some streets altogether and speeds were kept low on others to avoid the occasional fringe-topped carriage pulled by the original horse power. A golden sun radiated goodwill in an azure Southern sky.

Life could be good…would be good again, he reminded himself. Someday.

"Sir?"

He looked up to see Katie poke her head anxiously around the corner in response to his buzzing her. "What did I do now?"

She was still with him after a week. Personnel had failed to find an executive assistant that suited him. It wasn't that Holly hadn't tried. She'd sent three candidates up to him for interviews after she'd screened dozens of others. None of them had seemed right to him.

He wondered if he was unconsciously seeing faults in the candidates that didn't exist. Yet he'd been so sure he wanted Katie out from underfoot. She was turning his world upside down.

She made it impossible for him to concentrate on important decisions. He was always too aware of her body—the way she settled one hip lower than the other when she was retrieving a file for him. The way she sat, so very straight, which tended to emphasize her small, nicely shaped breasts. The way she ran the tip of her tongue along her top lip as she took notes.

How was a man supposed to concentrate? He'd never had this problem with clerical help before!

"It's nothing to do with you, Katie. This time." He closed his eyes and pinched the bridge of his nose.

She let out a long, laborious sigh he half expected was for show. "That's a relief."

But when he looked up to find a decidedly guilty look on her face he wondered what she'd done that he hadn't yet discovered. Three days ago, she had rearranged every stick of furniture in his office...all by herself. Even the massive desk. She'd shown him the plastic slider contraptions, like little sleds, she'd used under the furniture legs. Katie told him the arrangement was now much more feng shui.

And just yesterday she'd brought him an English muffin with jam instead of his usual bagel and cream cheese with his coffee. Less fattening, she'd claimed. As if what he put in his body was her business! Who knew what she'd dream up next.

"Did you call me for a reason?"

"Yes." He stood up and paced the carpet, vaguely remembering an old game he'd played with his cousins...stepping only on the Aubusson's flowers, avoiding the leaves. *Fell in the drink!* they'd all shout when one of them slipped. Why was he thinking of silly childhood games now? "Maybe there's something you can help me with."

"Really?"

He winced at her exuberance. He'd pretty much avoided giving her anything important to do for him because she seemed compelled to tackle every task in a dangerously creative way.

"Yes. Come in and sit down." He waved her to a chair, then found his gaze locked on her long legs as she crossed the room. She wasn't a tall woman, but she gave the impression of height because she possessed a slim torso and limbs that seemed breathtakingly endless. He looked away. "I'm in rather a jam."

"Oh?"

"Yes. Tonight at Twin Oaks, my father's country club, there will be a banquet to benefit the homeless of Savannah and the surrounding region. It's been planned for months. My attending...well, the entire family making an appearance is crucial to my father's campaign. Nicola feels that a show of solidarity is in order, and I agree.''

"So?" Katie crossed her legs. His heart stopped.

"So—" He cleared his throat and turned toward the window, away from the accidental glimpse he'd gotten of the little wedge of shadow between her thighs. But he broke a sweat. "So, my date for the evening has just called and canceled.''

There was a long pause that forced him to turn back to her. She was frowning up at him as she tugged at the hem of her skirt. The same straight, black cotton skirt she'd worn nearly every day.

"Are you asking me to go with you? To be your date?"

He laughed nervously. This was a bad idea, he thought belatedly. "Well, not so much date as escort, you see—to round out the table.''

Her eyes darkened to the deepest jade, and he sensed a storm coming on though he felt helpless to predict the reason.

She said, "This is a formal sort of bash?"

He hesitated, cautious. "Yes."

She pursed her lips. "And you'll be wearing—?"

"A tux," he supplied impatiently. "Look, can you come with me or not?" He tried to lighten the mood. "Hey, it's a free meal.''

She stood up and took three long-legged, unconsciously sultry strides directly toward him. She placed her hands on his shoulders and leveled him with a solemn gaze. "You have enormous nerve, Mr. Danforth.''

He staggered backward. "All I did was ask you to accompany me to a very respectable party!"

"Men!" she huffed, her eyes glowing, cheeks afire. "Men like you with money and important positions, you think you can run everyone's life."

Now where was this coming from? Clearly, his invitation wasn't the real reason for this emotional outburst. Who had set her on edge this way?

He tried a conciliatory smile on her. "Ms. O'Brien, I didn't intend to offend. I just thought you might enjoy—"

"You thought I might like tagging along after you in your spiffy designer tux, me in my thrift-store polyester. Is that it?"

He was astonished. "I'm sorry. I guess I don't quite understand."

"Of course you don't." She flashed him a look of extreme annoyance. "How can you ask one of your employees to dress for society on what you pay them?"

"Technically, I don't pay you at all," he said. "The temp agency pays you."

She waved this off, lifted a finger and aimed it at his chest like a pistol. "Which is even less than your full-time clerical, I've checked. That's not the point. You expect a woman earning two dollars over minimum wage to shell out a couple thousand for a gown to wear for one night?"

He didn't stop to think where she might have shopped to see four-figure price tags. He was too busy with his defense. "That doesn't seem fair," he admitted. "I'm sorry. Really, Katie. Forgive me. Forget I ever asked."

She blinked at him then let her eyes drift down to the carpet and ran a toe across a peony. "No big deal."

Instant meekness. "How much are they getting a plate?"

"A thousand."

"Pretty good. I hope they raise a lot of money. No one should be without a home." She started out of his office, then seemed to have second thoughts. "And I hope you find someone who can afford to go with you."

Before she could reach the door to the outer office, he came up behind her.

"Wait." He touched her shoulder.

When she turned and looked up at him, a river of heat flowed through his body. It was so unexpected, so unwanted, yet potent and paralyzingly real, he couldn't speak for several seconds.

"Yes, sir?"

"I...wait just a minute, will you? Let me make a quick call."

Ten minutes later he was off the phone, having booked an appointment at the poshest dress salon in the city, took Katie by the arm and was guiding her toward the elevator.

"This is ridiculous," she moaned.

"It's all for a good cause," he responded. "I'm buying."

Besides, the idea of Katie in a clingy strapless number was definitely an intriguing one—and not to be missed, whatever the cost.

Katie strolled into Twin Oaks ballroom on Ian's arm and looked around nervously. It wasn't as if appearing at a party attended by hundreds of the socially elite was new to her. What terrified her were the photographers wending their way through the glittering crowd. All it would take was one wire-service photo that made its way back to Arizona, and she'd be found out. A change in hair color and style wouldn't be enough to fool her family.

She kept her head down as Ian led her across the room, past a young man wielding a digital camera.

"What's wrong?" Ian asked.

"Nothing, I just don't feel right without my glasses. I shouldn't have left them at home." They were sort of hokey as disguises went, but she felt more exposed without them.

"You said you could see fine without them. Just for reading, right?"

"Yes, but—"

"You look great without them," he whispered so close to her ear it made her shiver. "I'm surprised you didn't switch to contacts years ago."

She shrugged. If he ever looked at the lenses, he'd see they were clear glass.

"And the dress is stunning," he added.

Her gown did seem to be attracting attention among the guests. She'd chosen a gorgeous red georgette, ankle-length dress with spaghetti straps. As backless as a dress could be without flaunting the law. The owner of the salon where Ian had taken her insisted that the right red with her auburn hair would be magnificent. Apparently the man knew his colors. Every head turned as they passed.

"Thank you for the compliment," she said, meaning it, "and for the lovely dress. I do like it." Although now, under the lingering gaze of hundreds of eyes, she wondered if she should have selected something more subtle. But how could any woman pass up the perfect red dress?

"Good. It suits you."

She sensed he was holding back, keeping his comments relatively impersonal. Perhaps feeling awkward about their relationship now that it had wandered, albeit for practical reasons, outside of the office.

"Tell me what I'm supposed to do, other than smile and eat," she said.

"That's about it. I'll introduce you to the family. We have two tables reserved. My father will make a statement regarding our responsibility as citizens to care for our own—the homeless, those without jobs, children in need of support outside of their families. All good causes the Danforths have always championed."

She looked up at him. His expression was solemn, and genuine sadness touched his words. She believed he really did feel for the less fortunate.

Katie had been raised with the same ideals. She was proud of the Fortunes' contributions to society. "Then your father wants voters to know he's committed to solving the homeless problem?"

Ian nodded firmly. "That's why we're here."

From that moment on, she made spreading the word on Abraham's dedication her mission for the evening.

The speakers were thankfully brief. Abraham Danforth's simple but eloquent plea to the elite of Savannah rang with the generosity of a great man. Katie was impressed, and she could see in Ian's eyes an appreciation for his father, as if he, too, was learning about the man like the others in the room.

The food was delicious and nearly worth the price of a seat at the beautifully decorated tables. After dinner everyone was on their feet, mixing, chatting, milling about. Katie moved with Ian through the room, greeting people. When the topic of conversation threatened to turn to the Danforths' recent troubles, Katie deftly steered the group back toward the reason for the gala.

"Where did you learn to be such a diplomat?" Ian whispered as he took her hand and drew her into a corner away from the crowd and the orchestra. The hour was growing late, but she still felt fresh and excited.

Hadn't her parents and grandparents hosted fundraisers all of her life? Hadn't she been groomed to the social life? But she couldn't tell Ian that. She came up with a half-truth.

"With two bossy brothers, you learn to make peace or get clobbered."

He laughed. "I can't believe your parents would have actually allowed them to hit you."

"Oh, they wouldn't. My brothers learned early that so much as raising a hand to a girl was forbidden and resulted in swift punishment. But they found other ways to make my life miserable."

"Are they all still in Arizona?"

The question took her by surprise. "I...well, yes, my brothers never left."

"I'd like to meet the O'Brien boys someday," he said, with a rare smile. "What are their names?"

This was verging on dangerous territory. She didn't want to lie to Ian, but she was already caught up in her own deception, and there seemed no easy way out of it.

A shift in the crowd opened her view of the room. Abraham was walking past a couple of tables near the rear when a man reached out and stopped him with a tug on his sleeve. There was something demanding, almost threatening in the gesture. He was smiling tightly, speaking to Abraham, and she felt Ian's father tense from clear across the room.

"Who is that?" she asked.

Ian followed her gaze. "Talking to my father?"

"Yes. Him and the guy seated beside him."

Ian's eyes narrowed as he studied the scene. "How did *they* get in here?" he muttered.

"Who?"

"Jaime Hernandez is a Colombian coffee supplier. The man with his hand on Dad's arm is Ernesto Escalante. He's been trying to pressure me into buying from Hernandez."

"Why would he do that?" she asked, even as he started moving between tables across the room.

"That's the question. From the information we've gathered, I'm pretty sure Escalante is a major mover in a cartel that deals in controlled substances."

"You mean he's a drug lord?"

"Yes. And if he's hoping to use Danforth & Danforth to launder his dirty money, he's going to be disappointed."

They were already halfway across the room. The crowd had thinned considerably in the past hour, making it easier to move. Ian broke into a jog, and Katie picked up her skirt and ran to keep up with him.

"Why don't you tell them to go away?" she asked breathlessly as they rounded a table.

"We have. They won't."

She shivered at the stormy look in Ian's eyes. Impulsively she grasped his hand, trying to slow him down.

"Wait. Are they dangerous?"

He kept moving, dragging her along with him. "I

don't know. But they don't belong here, and they're about to leave.'' He shook off her hand. ''Stay here.''

Katie swallowed as she watched him cross the last twenty feet in long strides. It wasn't that she thought Ian couldn't handle himself. And Abraham, the combat veteran of an earlier generation, was a man who wouldn't back down from any confrontation. But she couldn't let whatever might happen next attract the interest of the press. As much for Abraham's sake as for her own.

A reporter could twist an incident like this in the most obscene direction. *Honest Abe II Parties with Drug Lords!* His campaign was bound to suffer.

She looked around quickly and located a tall, serious looking man she was sure must be one of the security team employed for the function. Dressed in a rental tux to blend with the crowd, he didn't appear to have noticed the potential trouble. She'd made friends with her father's private guards as a child. During her teenage years, they'd sometimes looked the other way when she wanted to sneak out and visit a girlfriend.

Katie walked up to him and whispered a few words. Seconds later, he had communicated by radio with three other fellows with no discernible necks. They moved in quickly around the Danforths and the Colombians.

''Anything we can do, sir?'' the senior of the squad asked casually.

Ian looked around, as if surprised then relieved. ''My father was just suggesting these gentlemen might find the rest of the evening a little tame for their taste in entertainment.''

The Colombians looked at Ian, then Abraham, then the guards. ''We're supporting a good cause by being here," Escalante said, stubbing out his cigar. "The band is quite good. Our ladies like to dance." He winked at the two young women in sequined gowns who sat at their table.

"We're here to raise money for the unfortunate," Ian said coldly. "If you want to talk business, make arrangements with my office. My father is no longer actively involved in the company's operating decisions."

"Ah, too bad," Hernandez said, his eyes bright and black. He laughed. "They put you out to pasture, Grandpa?"

Abraham was about to respond angrily but Ian put his hand on his father's arm. "Don't, Dad."

Katie held her breath until the elder Danforth took a step back, though his face was a rigid mask of anger.

"Another meeting would accomplish nothing," Ian stated. "I've already told you, we won't be purchasing from you, Mr. Hernandez. Mr. Escalante knows my reasons."

"I'm disappointed to hear that," Hernandez said, standing beside Escalante. He was a short man, but his hands were massive, their backs ridged with muscle as if he'd used them hard all of his life.

Nevertheless, it was Escalante who struck Katie as the more dangerous of the two. His dark, glittering eyes never ceased moving, taking in the whole room, gauging every movement—close or far. And he never stopped smiling.

"Maybe, for reasons of their own, my good friend's competitors will drop out of the race. Then you will need to buy his coffee beans to stay in business," Escalante said. "You won't have a choice."

Katie held her breath. Abraham looked as if he was

about to explode, but Ian stepped in front of his father. "If anyone withdraws their bid for our business, we'll know why," Ian warned, his eyes narrowed, the muscles along the sides of his neck taut. "There are laws against your kind of strong-arm tactics."

Katie laid a hand on his arm when he took a step toward the two men. The security guards took their cue and moved in closer.

For several heartbeats, the tension hung thick and prickly about them, and Katie literally held her breath. At last, the two Colombians stepped away from the table and signaled their dates to join them.

"We will be in touch," Escalante said, still smiling.

Katie's heart raced painfully, and her skin crawled as she watched the foursome leave the room, escorted by two of the security guards. The muscles beneath the straps of her gown burned with strain, and she gave each shoulder a little roll to loosen them.

Abraham looked around the room, as if to reassure himself that the press hadn't witnessed any of what had just happened. Luckily, the photographers seemed to have left by then.

"You won't let them in, Ian," Abraham murmured as he watched them disappear through the ballroom doorway.

"No, sir. We have a legitimate reason for not dealing with them. Their product isn't up to our standards."

"Good. Stick to your guns." Abraham turned to Katie. "Thank you, my dear, for having the good sense to round up reinforcements." He smiled graciously. "It's always best to have the numbers on your side."

Ian opened the door for Katie and stepped back to let her inside her apartment. The Colombians' appearance at the gala had chilled the spirit of the festivities. He had left as soon as he sensed Abraham didn't need him anymore.

"You must be exhausted," he told Katie, handing back the keys to her.

She smiled at him over her shoulder and pirouetted across the modest living room, red georgette fluttering about her ankles. "Not at all. I'm still all charged up!"

He supposed she was pretending for his benefit. He felt utterly drained. "I'm sorry about that scene. It spoiled a good party."

"No, it didn't. I thought it was rather exciting, ac-tu-al-ly." Her final word seemed to require a good deal of concentration to correctly complete it. The trajectory of her stroll across the living room swerved a few feet north of the couch. She turned, stepped to her left and plopped down on the middle cushion with a grin. "Great party!"

"You had way too much champagne in the last half hour before we left," he said, shutting the apartment door behind him. He wanted to make sure she'd be all right before he took his leave. "Can I make you some coffee?"

She lifted a delicate hand and waved it at him in polite refusal. "No need. By the by, you and your father make a killer team."

She was intentionally changing the subject, but he was intrigued and didn't call her on it. "How is that?" He'd never thought of himself as good enough for Abraham's team, whatever the job. Most of his childhood had been spent trying to prove himself to a man who was rarely around.

When Abraham handed over Danforth & Danforth

Import Company to him, Ian had been genuinely surprised, even though it was traditional for the eldest son to take the reins when the father retired. Of course, this had happened all the sooner because of Abraham's political aspirations.

Katie made a pleased sound in her throat halfway between a sigh and a purr. "I tell you...the fire in both your eyes was enough to make any party crasher slink away." She tapped the cushion beside her on the couch. "Have a seat. You deserve a rest."

He focused on the right shoulder strap of her dress, which had slipped down her arm. Even when properly supported, the scooped bodice revealed an enticing décolleté. He wasn't sure that bringing himself closer to that part of her anatomy would be wise.

He sat anyway. And enjoyed the view.

"You know," she said, letting her head drop back and eyes drift closed, "you don't make a bad boss at all."

"Thank you." He wasn't absolutely sure she was drunk. Perhaps this was just one of her playful moods. Either way, he felt caution was advisable. "You don't make a bad assistant."

"Liar." She laughed.

Ian smiled at her. "Well, you haven't had much time to practice. I expect you'll learn. One day you'll be a top-notch EA." He studied her for a moment. Her eyes were still shut, and she was smiling at something. "Or something far more challenging. Tell me about yourself, Katie."

"You have my résumé."

"I mean, who are you really? Tell me about your family and growing up in Arizona. I've never been there."

Her eyelids flickered open suddenly, and she stared at him, suddenly sober. "I had a family like anyone else. It was really a very boring childhood."

He slowly shook his head. "No. There's something different about you. Something polished and fine." He touched an auburn lock that had separated itself from the tumble of curls over her shoulders. "And mysterious."

Her laugh this time was forced. "That's ridiculous."

He leaned toward her. "So why did you turn your face away or duck into the ladies' room whenever a photographer came our way tonight? Why are you so worried about having your picture taken?"

"I've just always been sensitive about my appearance," she said defensively.

"I don't believe that for a minute. You look sensational, and you know it."

She stiffened and flashed her eyes at him. "Maybe you should leave now. I'm tired."

But he was just getting started. He'd hit a nerve, and he sensed that if he pushed just a little harder he'd discover what it was that made Katie O'Brien seem so special. And why she wanted to hide it.

"I'll leave, if you tell me three things I don't already know about you."

She rolled her eyes, groaned and dropped her head back against the couch cushions in an exaggerated posture of defeat. "You want to play guessing games? All right, you win." She viewed him slyly through a screen of long lashes. "But you have to follow the same rules. I tell you three secrets, and you tell me three things I haven't already discovered about you."

He wasn't sure he liked the second part of the bargain, but if it was the price he had to pay... "You first."

"Fine." She thought for a moment, and he got the clear sense that she was eliminating information she felt uncomfortable sharing. "I hate asparagus."

"Not personal enough," he objected. If she was going to play cat and mouse with him, he was damn well going to be one aggressive feline.

"I take asparagus very personally!" She huffed at him when he leveled an uncompromising gaze her way. "Oh, all right. My father was in construction...how's that?"

"I'm not sure that counts, since you already told me that. But I'll let it go this time," he said generously.

She grinned. "Thanks. Now you."

"The estate where I grew up, Crofthaven, has a ghost."

"No." She laughed. "I thought you were just kidding about that."

"Honest, it does. We've all seen her, one time or another."

"Her? You can tell it's a woman?"

"Absolutely."

"I'd love to meet her." She sat up straight, her eyes no longer the least bit sleepy looking. They shone with rich variegated greens he'd only seen one clear day when he'd been vacationing on the Adriatic Sea. He moved closer, intrigued by their brightness.

"My theory is," he began again slowly, "she only appears to people she feels might help her. Mostly family members."

"Help her do what?"

"We're not sure what she's asking us to do," he said.

"She talks?" Katie unconsciously did the trick he liked so well with the tip of her tongue along her upper lip, and it totally unsettled him.

He nodded but couldn't take his eyes off her mouth, which was so very expressive when she was concentrating. "She says something, although it's difficult to understand her. All I've ever gotten is something about needing to go home. And once, I thought I heard the word *farther*."

"Wow." She looked thoughtful. "That was a good one. Now I can't hold back." She took a deep breath. "Okay. My family lives in the desert. It's very beautiful. Not many people know that. They think of the desert as something dangerous and uncomfortable and ugly. But it isn't at all."

"Tell me what it's like." The urge to connect with her in a way other than words was irresistible. He rested his hand over hers, but she didn't seem to notice.

"After it rains, the cacti bloom. The flowers are the color of sunshine—orange, red, yellow and gold. It's as if they've been sleeping, soaking up all that brightness and waiting to give it back on the first rainy day."

Her words quickened as her voice grew more excited. "And there are caverns at the edge of town on the Native American reservation. They say they're enchanted, have mystical powers."

"No!" he said, mimicking her.

She laughed at him. "Really. That's where my parents fell in love. My dad's part Indian, so I guess I am, too." She met his eyes with pride.

"Go on," he said, sensing there was more.

"It's impossible to imagine the desert without ever having been there. The light in the morning is pure and brilliant, like reflections cast by a crystal. I can't explain it. Artists come from all over to paint there.''

''Sounds amazing,'' he whispered, stroking her fingers as they rested in her lap.

''It is. I've never seen a ghost there, not even in the caverns. But you can feel the spirits of people long gone when you step inside the dark cool spaces of the caverns. You stand very still, close your eyes and they're there.'' She let her eyelids drift down as if to demonstrate.

God, she's beautiful, Ian thought.

Before he could draw a next breath, he found his lips touching hers. It happened. Just happened without his consciously leaning into her, although he must have. Her words so moved him, her simple sweetness compelled him.

Katie's eyes fluttered open as their kiss ended, and she looked at him but said nothing.

Quickly he sat back, making space between them. ''Go on,'' he said. ''Tell me more.''

She looked at their hands, his larger one covering hers, then up at his eyes again, plaintively. ''That's all. I don't think I can play this game anymore.''

Perhaps she had revealed more to him than she'd intended. ''Don't quit now,'' he begged her.

''But that was so personal. I don't talk about such things to anyone.'' She looked more amazed at herself than upset with him.

''All right,'' he said quickly. ''I'll have to match the intimacy of your revelations, just to be fair.''

He mentally weeded out facts he was sure she knew from perusing company files. He'd noticed she'd taken an interest in scanning material as she returned it to its proper drawer.

"I had a son." His heart shuddered at the realization of what had just passed through his lips. How had that come out? Why now...and to her?

She stared at him. "You were married?"

"A long time ago. I was too young, so was she."

"And the baby?"

He didn't answer. Couldn't even meet her inquiring expression. He felt her hand turn, fingertips lace between his and her palm settle with comforting warmth against his.

"It's all right, Ian. This is a silly game. We shouldn't have started it. If you don't want to—"

"No," he said. "I'm fine. It's been a long time, after all."

Katie moved closer to him on the couch, their hips touching. She brought her hand, holding his, more deeply into her lap, as if to cradle this small part of him. As if by tenderly soothing his fingers, palm, wrist, she could console the whole of him.

"So tell me about your son," she murmured.

The razorlike pain slashed through him. It was easier to forget. "He died."

"Oh, Ian, I'm so sorry."

And now he couldn't stop. The pain that never left spurred him on. "He was...never really born. It was a miscarriage at five months, but we knew he was a boy from the sonograms. He'd been growing, seemed healthy according to the doctor. Something just...went wrong."

"A son," she breathed.

"I would have felt the same had it been a girl," he rasped out in anguish.

"Of course," she whispered, stroking his hand that had tightened into a fist.

The terrible memories had tumbled around like coffee beans in a roaster all these years. He held in the pain, cherishing it, making it a selfish thing. At least the hurt was something to hold on to after his baby and his wife were gone. Pain was sometimes better than having nothing at all.

For the first time, though, he was sharing it.

Katie sat quietly, listening. When he paused, her silence encouraged him to let go of more.

"We were just out of college. My girlfriend was dedicated to her new career. Both of us were beginning to find our way in the adult world. The pregnancy was an accident. Neither of us had wanted it. But once it happened I saw no alternative but for us to marry and give the baby a proper home."

"She didn't agree?" Katie whispered.

"No. She was very upset. A baby didn't fit her plans at all. But I talked her into getting married and keeping the child. I promised I'd give her all the support she needed to continue her career. We'd hire a nanny, and I'd alter my own schedule as necessary to be with the baby when conflicts arose." He grimaced at the ache in his heart. The guilt never left. "I should never have pushed her to it, but she agreed."

"But you loved each other?" Katie asked.

Ian had to think about this. "At the time, I thought so. But I'm not sure now. Clearly there wasn't enough love to hold us together after the miscarriage. Lara hadn't wanted to start a family yet, but losing the baby was a heartbreaking experience for her. And I'd imagined myself a father. I'd made the emotional leap. When the baby died in her womb, I...I—" He had still wanted to be a father.

Katie squeezed his hand, and a healing radiance

seemed to pass into him through their touching palms, soothing his shattered soul.

She snuggled closer to him, laid her cheek against his shoulder. "Maybe he wasn't ready to be born yet," she murmured.

Her comment puzzled him. "What?"

"Maybe," she said, "the little fellow needed to wait for the right mom." The innocence of her words touched him. "*You* were ready, Ian, but the woman carrying him was not."

It didn't make a bit of sense, biologically. He knew that. She probably did, too. Maybe it was that ancient, tribal mysticism of her ancestors coming through. Maybe these things just couldn't be explained. At best, they could only be endured.

"Perhaps you're right." He touched his lips to the soft auburn curls atop her head, grateful for this night.

Katie shifted against him as if preparing to stand up. He felt indebted to her. He felt closer to her than he'd felt to any other human being. Ever. What had prompted him to reveal his innermost pain to a simple office clerk?

Or had she already become more than that?

Katie had smoothed countless shaky social interactions at the gala. She'd supported his family in a volatile confrontation with the cartel. And now she'd lessened his pain.

"Ian?"

He turned to her. If possible, her eyes had grown brighter. "Yes?"

"Kiss me again. Please."

This is a mistake, his inner voice told him. Kissing her on impulse was one thing, but kissing her deliberately was totally inappropriate.

He was concocting a witty retort, a tactful excuse
with which to escape, when she curled her knees beneath her, swiveling on the cushion, and pinned his
face between her two small hands. She planted her lips
firmly over his.

There isn't a man on earth who can say no to this,
the same voice said. Damn right, he thought, and
kissed her back.

Ian wrapped his arms around her, bringing her
against his chest, pinning her tiny frame to his, even
though she gave not the least hint of struggle.

Time stopped. The world dropped away, and he with
it. All consciousness of the details of life were swept
away, like a storm blowing clean, fresh air over the
ravished land. He felt only her. Knew only Katie.

Ian's lips found her throat, then her cheek, the
tender indentation of flesh at her temple, her mouth
again and again. It seemed impossible to stop kissing
her. Everywhere. Impossible, too, to keep his hands
quietly on her back. They'd begun to wander to places
soft and warm and hidden beneath her gown but inti-
mately definable by touch.

Her breasts, her waist, the lush fullness of her hips.

At last out of breath, he turned his head to one side
and squeezed his eyes shut, trying to clear his thoughts
just long enough to stop acting on impulse and understand what was happening.

"Ian?" Her voice quivered.

He hoped to God he hadn't embarrassed or upset
her. "Yes?"

"It's all right. I understand."

"You do?"

She shifted gently out of his arms, and he ached to

pull her back into his embrace. But he restrained himself.

"It's a terrible thing to lose a child," she whispered. "You needed this…to be touched by someone. To remember life goes on."

"I'm sorry if I—"

She pressed two fingers across his lips. "Hush. It's forgotten. And now I need to get some sleep."

"Of course. Thank you, Katie, for tonight."

Still under the spell of her, still reeling from the sensations of her body pressed to his, he deliberately walked out her apartment door. He took the elevator down to his car, climbed into the driver's seat but didn't start the engine.

For a very long time he sat there, trying to figure out if she was right. Had he just needed someone—anyone—to hold him? Or had he stumbled over feelings, hungers, desires far too complex and way too hot for him to handle?

Five

By Wednesday of the next week, Katie was nearly beside herself. Neither she nor Ian had mentioned those breathless, confusing, delicious moments at her apartment following the gala. In fact, to any outside observer, their working relationship would have seemed absolutely proper and detached.

But in her heart, Katie knew that something powerful had happened that night, and it had changed them both.

That was why she was afraid.

Terrified, really, because as much as she liked and admired Ian for being strong in the face of thugs and for blaming himself when a baby that was never meant to be born didn't have a chance to draw a single sweet breath, as much as she believed he was a very good man, and as deeply as she'd been touched by him...she knew it would be her ruin to let herself fall in love with him.

Why?

Because, she answered her own question, *he's too much like all the men in my family.*

It was true. Ian Danforth had grown up in a privileged world. Although she was fascinated by his worldliness, at least some of it due to his being thirteen years older than she (she had peeked at his file), she knew what men like Ian did to their women. They controlled them.

Not always cruelly, though. Her father was never mean to her mother or to her. He clearly adored both of them. But sometimes his love came too close to smothering her. And her mother often seemed to make the situation worse by siding with him.

Her parents had orchestrated every facet of her life, from choosing her childhood friends to selecting a college for her and dictating what she did after she graduated. Which was mostly stay near home and prepare to marry. They'd made numerous blatant and embarrassing attempts to match her with some of the Southwest's most eligible bachelors. No doubt with good intentions. They wanted her to be safe and happy, to provide them with lots of grandchildren and never have to worry about how to feed them.

She had balked…and eventually run.

She wasn't about to leap out of that pot straight into Ian Danforth's fire.

This was her life, and she would live it her way.

Meanwhile, though, she wasn't sure how she'd continue functioning around the man in his office. Every time he entered her work area, she imagined his arms closing around her, the intensity of his kisses, the yearning telegraphed through every muscle and sinew of his hard body.

Even now, just remembering, she became a puddle.

"Ms. O'Brien?"

"Huh? I mean...yes, sir?" She stared at the intercom on her desk, but the call button wasn't lit. A subtle movement caught the corner of her eye, and she turned with a start at the appearance of a sandy-beige pant leg beside her chair.

"Are you all right?" Ian asked. "I've been buzzing you."

"Sorry. I was preoccupied." Katie turned away, unsettled by the proximity of his zipper, eye level. She felt herself go hot in the cheeks, and stifled a jittery giggle. *Grow up,* she told herself.

But when she did manage to meet Ian's rich hazel eyes, her heart thrummed in answer to them. *Steady, girl!*

How she wished Katie, the real Katie O'Brien, were still in town. She would be able to talk her out of this insane infatuation. Katie might come up with devil-may-care plots, like this switching identity thing, but she could be very levelheaded about men. Her friend would remind her why she'd left home in the first place, and of all she had to gain by remaining independent.

Wasn't the real Katie having the time of her life in Europe this very moment? Free as a bird. Doing as she pleased. No man to tell her she should be doing one thing when she wanted to do another.

Katie straightened up and folded her hands on the desk, pretending composure. "Yes, sir. What can I do for you?"

Ian scowled down at her, looking vaguely befuddled by her behavior. "Have the newspapers arrived yet?"

"No, sir. Are you expecting anything special in them?"

"One of the reporters at the gala mentioned she thought her article on the homeless would run in today's paper. I want to see it as soon as possible, in case we need to run damage control on behalf of my father."

"I'll bring them to you as soon as they arrive." She reached for a file, feigning involvement in a critical task when he didn't immediately leave.

"Katie," he said.

She didn't look up. Please, God, don't let him ask about that night! "Yes?" She held her breath, but after a moment he just sighed.

"Never mind. I'll be in my office."

"Right." She heard his door close and only then released the breath she'd been holding.

The papers had arrived. The *Savannah Morning News, Washington Post, New York Times, Saint Louis Dispatch, L.A. Times, Houston Chronicle* and *Wall Street Journal.* Seven arrived every day, delivered by a local news service.

Ian tracked business and political news in all areas of the country where D&D's coffee shops were located. Although he had a clipping service for any direct mention of the company or the family, he liked a broader picture of their shops' communities.

Katie thanked the deliveryman and pulled out the Houston paper, which was the one nearest her own hometown. She checked every day, just in case.

The headline warned of oil prices skyrocketing.

Nothing new there. She shrugged and was about to turn to the society pages when a photo just below the fold on the front page caught her eye, and she nearly shrieked.

Her…it was her!

The professional photo had been taken on the eve of her "coming out" in Tucson. Her natural dark brown hair was arranged in a sophisticated coif on top of her head. The white satin bodice hugged her torso but revealed bare shoulders. A string of pearls—her grandmother's—clasped delicately around her throat.

If she hadn't been left gasping for breath at the sight of the photo, the caption beneath would have done the job: Disappearing Heiress Spotted In Bus Station!

Oh no, no, no…

Katie went numb. She gripped the top of the desk for support. Her heart in her throat, she read quickly, soaking up word after horrifying word.

The article quoted a man who believed he had seen a young woman matching her description in the Greyhound terminal in downtown Saint Louis—the very one she'd passed through on her way across the country to Georgia. The time and date matched her two-hour layover there.

Katie's stomach lurched. Her heart flip-flopped in her chest, unable to find a steady beat.

Without thinking twice, she stuffed the *Chronicle* into her top desk drawer, then hastily scanned the other papers. Nothing about her in them yet. Maybe this would be the end of it. Maybe other editors would find much more important stories to cover, and soon even the southwestern papers would forget about her.

She delivered Ian's stack of crisp newsprint to him. He glanced up at her, but she turned and hastily walked away, hoping he wouldn't notice he was short one city.

"Wait."

Katie bit down on her lower lip. She poked her eyeglasses back up the bridge of her nose and came around to face him again.

"Is something wrong, Katie?"

"No. Nothing." She produced a wobbly smile.

"You look awfully pale."

She lifted one shoulder. "Just tired, I guess." She forced herself to walk calmly back to her desk and sit down, when she felt like running from the building.

It wasn't just being discovered that worried her. She was thinking about her parents and the rest of her family. Not until this moment had it struck her how worried they might be about her.

The article had included an emotional quote from her father: "If someone out there has our daughter, please know that we'll do anything, give anything they require to return her to us."

Did they think she'd been kidnapped? Hadn't they found the note she'd left in her room telling them she'd needed to be on her own? Assuring them she'd be all right?

Then later in the article, her father's attorney: "Katherine, if you're able to contact us, please do. Your parents only want to see you safely home again."

Safely home again. Wasn't that the point?

She didn't want to be protected, to be made safe like a helpless child when what she needed was a life of her own! If she made mistakes, so be it—they would be hers to make!

Who in this world today could claim immunity from

strife? Life was unpredictable by its nature. Shouldn't she get used to facing challenges on her own?

As much as Katie longed to reassure her family that she was all right, she couldn't take that risk. Not yet. Once she'd proved to herself, and them, that she could do for herself, she'd tell them where she was.

In the meantime, perhaps she could come up with a way of communicating to them that she wasn't in danger. A way that wouldn't disclose her whereabouts— because she was certain that if her father and uncles ever found out where she was, they'd come after her and drag her home.

Ian barely glanced at the newspapers that morning. After quickly flipping through the stack to make sure nothing unsavory had been printed about Abraham or the family, he pushed them aside and stared out the expanse of tinted glass overlooking his beloved Savannah.

The view used to excite him. He could almost feel his heart pumping in time to the slow but steady rhythm of the city. He'd survived bitter disappointment and loss, much as this city had survived a bloody civil war, but only after sacrificing many of her sons. It was no small miracle that she hadn't been burned to the ground like other Southern cities. It seemed an equal miracle that he'd somehow struggled on after the loss of his son.

His work for the family company had kept him sane, kept him going, day after day. Then his father had stepped down, leaving Ian as CEO, and Ian had told himself that this would be enough. He'd dedicate his life to the firm, to growing Danforth & Danforth into one of the most powerful import businesses in the U.S.

But it wasn't enough. Not by a long shot. He knew that now.

It was all Katie O'Brien's fault.

She'd awakened him to the prospect of living again in the most provocative way. She'd enticed him, soothed him, made him sit up and take notice of her as an extraordinary, sexually desirable woman. She'd challenged him to look beyond his loss.

But he wasn't ready to do that...not yet. So he had to do something about her.

He had to separate himself somehow from her, regain his balance. As long as she was careening around his office, he was useless. Aside from her habit of moving the furnishings and questioning his directives, she made him think about doing wicked, delicious things to her.

And these things were the sort a man shouldn't even consider doing during work hours.

The company needed a CEO with both feet on the ground, his mind firmly on business. But Holly still hadn't found anyone suitable for a permanent EA, so maybe another temp was the answer.

He picked up his phone, hit the button for the outer office. "Katie, have you had lunch yet?"

"No, sir."

Damn, just hearing her voice set off a chain reaction of nerves that ended with fireworks in his lap. He shifted in his chair and tried to ignore them.

"I need to speak with you about something important. Would you mind taking lunch with me downstairs at the coffee shop?"

There was a moment's hesitation, as if she already suspected his motives. "Fine with me."

Ian hung up. It had to be done. There was no other way.

He hardly glanced at Katie as he whisked past her desk and through the door toward the elevator. Trusting that she followed, he hit the down button, waited, then strode through the doors the moment they swished open. He felt Katie's presence as she stepped in beside him, but didn't dare look directly at her.

She was trying to make eye contact, he could tell, but he wouldn't allow even this simple connection between them until they were safely in public view. There was a limit to how much temptation he could take.

They found a table and ordered—a seafood salad for her, a hearty burger with Swiss melting over it for him—and still he hadn't really looked at her. He bit into his burger, tasting nothing, chewed with a good show of concentration and enjoyment. At last, he shifted his attention from the food to her.

She was sitting very still. He noticed she hadn't touched her salad.

"Aren't you hungry?" he asked.

"You're going to fire me, aren't you?"

Her tone was heartbreaking. He cringed. "Katie, I'm not going to fire you."

"What then? Have I made some sort of awful mistake? Did I do something wrong? I like to handle things my way and that may not be your way, but I've gotten everything done that you asked, one way or another."

"Yes, you have." He pushed his plate away. The burger lay heavily in his stomach. "And your energy and dedication are deeply appreciated." Even though she had wreaked havoc on his ability to complete any work at all. "The thing is, a temporary clerical assistant is just that. We never expected you to be with us for more than a week, at most two."

"So you said the day I arrived. Are you telling me now that you've found a permanent EA?"

"Actually, no. But it's been over two weeks and I think it would be to your benefit as well as ours for you to move on."

Her face fell. "Leave Danforth & Danforth? But I like it here. I really do!"

"We try to make everyone feel like family here. I'm glad you've enjoyed being with us." He forced a smile, feeling like a creep for shoving her out. "But I think we might use the job you have now as a testing ground for candidates, you know, for the permanent position."

"I could do that," she said quickly. "Be your real executive assistant."

"No. No, you couldn't," he said cautiously.

"Why? I'm not good enough?"

"You need a little more experience, that's all."

"I could get it while I'm working for you. Everyone needs some training."

"I...you—" Dammit, was there any way to avoid saying the words? He looked around to make sure no one was within hearing distance. He whispered, "Katie, it was all my fault, what happened in your apartment. I should never have kissed you. I overstepped my boundaries as an employer."

Strangely, she looked suddenly brighter, then he saw the mischief in her eyes. "If you recall, sir, I was the one who kissed you the second time."

He glanced around once more, but the nearby tables

were empty and the level of chatter in the coffee shop was so high he was certain no one could hear them.

"I am very attracted to you," he confessed. "The fact is, I'm finding it damn difficult to get anything done with you around."

She beamed at him. "I thought it was just me."

"Pardon?"

"I thought maybe I was the only one attracted. I like you an awful lot, Ian."

"Katie, no."

"There's nothing wrong in that," she insisted. "What's awful is when one person does and the other doesn't."

He leaned farther over the table. "You're much too young for me."

"Rubbish." She smiled.

"I'm serious. And I've never dated an employee. I don't intend to start now."

"You already have. You took me to the gala."

"That wasn't a date."

"Fits my definition," she said cheerfully.

"Stop that!" Several heads turned at his raised voice, and Ian forced himself to speak more softly, despite his growing frustration. "The point is, I can't keep you in my office and have these thoughts about you."

"So," she said slowly, as if trying to understand, "you want me to leave the company so that we can start a serious romantic relationship?"

"No... I mean, I don't know." He groaned, stabbed a French fry with his fork and waved it at her. "You're putting words in my mouth."

"I'm just trying to understand what you expect of

me," she said much too calmly. Another ten minutes of this, and the woman would drive him insane.

"I don't expect anything of you," he said. "That's the point."

The shattered expression in her eyes nearly broke his heart. "You're telling me to go away, to get lost."

"Not get lost, as you put it. I'll give the temp agency a glowing recommendation for you, tell them we've filled the position. You'll go back to them and be reassigned, having had experience you can use in your next placement. And if you need references for future applications with other companies, I'll be glad to accommodate."

She didn't respond right away. She seemed intent upon the tips of her nails as she lightly drummed them on the tabletop. "I see." There was weight in her words. He didn't like the sound of them.

"You'll be fine," he assured her.

"And what about us?"

"I told you, there is no us."

If he ever again became seriously, romantically involved with anyone, it would be with a woman with as much inclination to produce and raise a family as he had. Katie, though attractive and energetic and fascinating in her own ways, wasn't ready to settle down.

He'd made that mistake once before. He'd paid dearly.

"We're very different, you and I." It sounded lame even to his own ears. "The age and all…"

"So you've said before." She pushed her salad away and stared out the window at passersby on the sidewalk.

"In all fairness, Katie," he said gently, reaching across the table to touch her hand, "I don't want to start something I can't see through to the right conclusion.''

Her head snapped around, sending red curls into disarray. ''Which is?''

''Marriage, a family, stability.'' He smiled weakly at her. ''I'm sorry, Katie. It just seems to me that you're set on trying your wings. And I'm past that stage of life. I need more than a fling. If we'd met at another time, under different circumstances—''

''Oh, please!'' she snapped, shooting to her feet. Her expression was stormy. Snatching her purse from the floor beside her chair, she set back her shoulders and looked down at him without an ounce of pride given away. ''Don't bother with clichés. I understand. You're right. I need something more, too.'' She turned and walked away.

It hurt. Ian's ditching her stung far worse than anything before in her life.

Not until he had begun his speech had it occurred to her how much staying at Danforth & Danforth meant to her. And how much she'd miss being around Ian.

It wasn't that she was in love with him, she told herself. He was cutting her off from the camaraderie she'd developed with him and with other employees over the past days. She'd felt part of a team. And, since the gala, part of a special and exciting family.

Hadn't she stood by the Danforths in a moment of crisis at the country club? And before that, when she'd sat in the First City Club with Abraham, Ian and Nicola? How amazing was that! Forget about the elite setting and the chef's delectable creations. She'd sat in on a prospective Senator's strategy session. She'd given her opinion and, amazingly, people had listened!

How often had she wished her own parents would take her seriously?

Damn Ian!

There was nothing she could do about his pushing her out of his personal life. But she'd be darned if she'd let Ian Danforth force her out of a job she loved.

She rushed down three flights of stairs, whirled like a human tornado into Holly's office and planted herself in the chair across from her desk. Holly was on the phone, but Katie was prepared to wait—no matter how long. Holly glanced up at her curiously as she hung up.

"Do I sense the fallout of Danforth temper?" She raised one brow. "I hope he didn't leave bruises."

"No visible marks." Katie sighed and slumped deeper in the chair. "I'm just the walking wounded in need of another job."

"I see. Then Ian didn't take my advice. He's asked you to leave."

"He told you he was going to do this?"

"Days ago," Holly admitted. "I suggested he wait until we'd found a permanent replacement."

"That son of a—"

"Katie, he's my boss," Holly interrupted quietly. "Our boss, until you officially leave here."

"Sorry. It's just that he's being so stubborn and selfish and—"

"Nothing I haven't heard about the man before," Holly said, reaching behind her for a folder from a chrome sorting rack. "But he's fair, means well, and he's brilliant at his job."

"I'm not debating the second two counts," Katie grumbled.

"So he's told you he definitely wants you out?"

"Yes." Katie felt so close to tears she could taste their salty warning. But she wouldn't cry. No, she would not. "The thing is, I really do like it here. It's a great place to work—everyone's so nice and helpful, and I'm learning so much."

Holly looked at her hard, then opened the folder and flipped pages. "Tell you what I'll do. There's an opening for an executive assistant to one of our district managers." She pointed to a name on the page. "I think you'd like her a lot. If you want, I'll submit your application along with the others. It's a permanent position, though—you'd have to leave the temp agency and commit at least a full year to us."

Katie glowed with hope. "Okay! But please don't tell Ian."

"I'm not sure I can do that." Holly nipped at her bottom lip thoughtfully. "Let's just say I'll wait a few days to break the news to him. Meanwhile, I think I can talk him into letting you stay another week to ten days. I'll assure him that we'll have his new EA by then." She hesitated, observing Katie solemnly. "Unless you don't think you can stand being around him that long."

"Oh, no." Katie beamed, feeling renewed confidence. "I can handle Ian Danforth just fine."

She left, humming. Ian might have won the first round, but she was determined to give him his money's worth in the second.

Six

D&D's was packed when Ian burst through its famous initial-embellished doors. He was furious. What the hell was Katie up to now?

He'd thought he had made himself clear the day before. But at noon when he'd finally made it into the office after a morning-long meeting, there she was at her desk.

"Holly would like you to call her," she said sweetly, as if he hadn't gently but firmly told her he no longer required her services a mere twenty-four hours earlier.

By the time he'd gotten off the phone with his personnel manager, Katie had left for lunch, and he'd been hot on her trail ever since. One of the clerks on the third floor told him she often ate with the office crowd in the first-floor coffee shop.

He spotted her sitting with four other women at a rear table.

"Afternoon, Mr. Danforth," a tall blonde said when he stopped behind Katie's chair. "Join us?"

"Not at the moment, thank you." He stepped to the side to face Katie. "Ms. O'Brien, I need to speak with you."

"I'm on my break," she said, taking a dainty bite of salad.

"It's important." The remark earned him glares from all around the table. Lunch was sacred. "Really important."

"Very well," Katie said pleasantly.

He controlled the urge to grab her by the scruff of her neck and drag her into the lobby, away from witnesses. Whether he'd kiss her or give her a good shake to bring her to her senses once he got her there, that was a toss-up. She headed for a less busy corner of the café, and he followed.

"Is there a problem with my morning's work?"

"No. There's a problem with your subversive tactics."

"Excuse me?" He could swear there was a touch of a smile on those expressive lips, but the rest of her face was perfectly blank.

"It means," he growled, "I thought we'd agreed yesterday that it was best for all concerned if you left the company."

"No-o-o." She extended the word as if to make herself clear to a recalcitrant toddler. "*You* decided it would be best if I no longer worked in your office. You said nothing about other positions in the company. Holly felt it would be all right for me to stay where I was just a few more days. It seemed the reasonable thing to do, since you need someone to cover the phone and all.''

He groaned. ''The point I thought I'd made clear was that after we'd—'' He lowered his voice. ''After we'd, you know—''

''Become intimate?'' she supplied innocently.

''Yes, that.'' How was it she could so easily fluster him? He had never been self-conscious about discussing sex before she showed up. ''I just didn't think it was right for us to be working together.''

''I agree.''

''You do?''

''Absolutely. That's why I've applied for a job in another department, on another floor.'' She smiled brightly at him. ''Holly says my chances look good.''

''She does, does she?'' he grumbled. This was getting more and more complicated. He felt as if he was losing control. Maybe he'd lost it a long time ago and just hadn't realized it. ''I still don't think it's a good idea.''

''I'm not sure you have any say in it,'' she stated calmly.

''Why shouldn't I? I'm CEO of the damn company!''

''Yes, but the personnel office does the hiring. You'd have to go out of your way to block my getting the job if I'm the most qualified.'' She tapped his chest with two fingers and smiled. ''I'm not sure that's legal, Mr. Danforth.''

He closed his eyes and thought evil, evil thoughts. The woman was right. It wouldn't be ethical for him to deny her a job if she deserved it.

''Besides,'' she continued, ''I couldn't very well leave you without an assistant. Holly is interviewing another list of applicants for your EA. Meanwhile, I'll just hold down the fort, as you say.''

He stared at her, feeling utterly defenseless. He had the distinct feeling the two women were ganging up on him, but it would sound paranoid to accuse them of plotting against him.

''Fine,'' he said with a long sigh. ''Another week or so. No big deal.'' He could handle temptation that long, couldn't he? And if she got the other job? He supposed he'd have to steer clear of her division...forever. ''I'll see you upstairs.''

He started to turn toward the elevators when he looked up to see two familiar figures crossing the foyer toward him, and he grinned, thankful for friendly faces.

''Wes...and Jasmine!'' Ian waved them over. ''How's the most beautiful reporter in all Savannah?'' Out of the corner of his eye, he sensed Katie tensing as she studied the elegant mocha-skinned woman who had swept his old friend Wesley off his feet.

''Hey, no flirting with my woman!'' Wes punched Ian lightly in the shoulder. ''They told me upstairs they saw you heading this way. I wanted to talk to you about that dot-com stock we discussed last week.'' He glanced curiously at Katie, who hadn't moved. ''But I don't want to interrupt you if you're busy.''

''Not at all. Katie O'Brien, this is Wesley Brooks and his fiancée Jasmine. Wes is my cousin's college roommate. Uncle Harold all but adopted Wes.''

''Very nice to meet you,'' Katie murmured. Now it was her turn to seem flustered, and he marveled at the sudden baffling change. She shot a nervous glance back at the coffee shop. ''I should go now. I have to finish lunch and get back to my desk.''

"You work here at Danforth's?" Jasmine asked.

"Ah, yes," Katie said, starting to back away from the group. "Just as a temp so far. But I'm hoping to stay."

"Well, good for you." Wes turned to Ian. "Actually, in addition to my data on that stock, Jasmine has news about your two party crashers at the gala."

Katie wheeled around, her green eyes suddenly bright with interest. "Maybe I could stay just a little while."

Ian gave her disparaging look but she ignored him. "Why don't we sit down over a cup. Sounds as if this might take a while." He motioned Wesley and Jasmine through the door into D&D's, and Katie trailed along. The table near the back where she had been sitting with her friends was now vacant, except for the remainder of her abandoned salad, so they settled there and ordered drinks.

"Go ahead, Jas," Ian said when they'd been served.

The attractive African-American reporter leaned over the table and spoke in a confidential tone.

"You asked me to help find out more about Escalante and Hernandez. The FBI are very interested in them, too. According to my source at the Bureau, these two are associated with one of the most powerful drug cartels in South America. You should be very careful, Ian. These are people with a history of playing very dirty."

"No surprise there," he muttered. "Have they turned up any evidence that these same folks might have been behind the bombing of our headquarters?"

"Not yet," Jasmine said, "but they haven't eliminated the possibility. What they do believe is that Escalante and Hernandez are part of a complex money-laundering scam on behalf of the cartel, which is why the pair is interested in Danforth & Danforth.''

Wesley nodded. ''Danforth's is an old, highly respected firm, above suspicion. That would make it very attractive to them as a means of turning drug money legitimate.''

''I'd wondered about that,'' Ian murmured, aware that Katie was drinking this all in, her eyes growing larger with every disturbing sentence. He wished to God she weren't there to hear this. He didn't want her involved in anything so dangerous. ''But the FBI can't act, I assume, until they have solid evidence?''

''Exactly,'' Jasmine responded. ''And my source has asked me to feel you out about helping with that.''

''How?'' he asked without hesitation. He lifted his cup to take a sip of the fragrant brew. It made sense the FBI wouldn't want Escalante to suspect he was working with the FBI. Jasmine was a clever go-between, in case the Colombians were watching him.

Jasmine stared at him solemnly. ''Meet with Escalante, in private.''

''Oh, Ian, no!'' Katie gasped, clutching at his arm. ''Jasmine, you just said they're violent men.''

Ian laid a hand over hers, but she quickly withdrew it, as if she realized her gesture was out of character for an employee. ''What sort of meeting?'' he asked.

Jasmine fished a business card from her purse. ''Call this agent. He's in charge of the investigation. He'll explain the details. I gather they hope to record a meeting between you and Escalante, get something on tape to incriminate him.''

Ian felt a rush of adrenaline at the thought. At last, after months of feeling helpless, he'd be able to do something concrete to stop these men and protect his employees and family.

"Maybe someone else could meet with them," Katie suggested, looking concerned.

"The only other person that would make sense is my father. And he can't do it."

"Why not?" Katie asked.

"The election. Honest Abe can't be seen meeting with anyone remotely associated with crime, even if it's to help the law. His enemies would find a way to make something of it."

"Ian's right," Jasmine murmured. "Politicians can twist the truth in ways you wouldn't imagine."

"It's settled. I'll make the call," Ian said.

A few minutes later, Katie sneaked a sideways glance at Ian as she walked beside him across the lobby. She was truly impressed by the man. Of course she worried about him cooperating with the FBI, but she respected the way he was standing up to criminals.

Ian motioned her ahead of him when the elevator door opened.

They stepped on. The paneling was of old oak, and the carpet a wine-red. She felt as if she was traveling in a plush antique train car.

"By the way," Ian said, as they zipped toward the fifth floor, "you seemed awfully edgy around Jasmine. What was that all about?"

"Nothing." She shrugged. "You're right, she really is beautiful. I love her taste in clothes."

"You're changing the subject."

"Well, talking to newspaper reporters makes me nervous."

"You were in the same room with a dozen or more

journalists at the gala.'' He narrowed his eyes and studied her suspiciously. ''It would seem you might have gotten used to them.''

In truth, she'd been terrified Jasmine might recognize her, connect her with the UPI photo. At the gala, she'd at first been terrified of being recognized. But as the evening continued she'd relaxed, realizing that with so many local celebrities on deck, the press was unlikely to be thinking about a lost debutante from a distant state.

But sitting across the table from a sharp-eyed investigative reporter, that was different. She had sensed that Jasmine was watching her every gesture, studying her as she spoke. Had the woman recognized her?

Ian seemed to be waiting for a response from her.

She grasped for the first thing that came to mind. ''It's just that—''

''Yes?'' he said.

''That woman should never wear blue with her coloring,'' Katie blurted out.

Ian laughed out loud and pushed through the door to his office with Katie close behind. ''I'll never understand women.''

''Not if we can help it,'' she mumbled beneath her breath, with a sense of relief.

''Don't accuse them of anything,'' the FBI agent warned. ''We don't want to put them on the defense.''

''Are you sure they won't know you've bugged my office?'' Ian asked.

Even though Katie stood half a room away from him, he could feel her tension. The odd thing was, he sensed her concern was more for him than for her own safety. He appreciated her loyalty, even after he'd done all he could to force her to leave Danforth's.

"We don't believe Escalante realizes we've made the connection between him and the cartel. That's in our favor. But if he suspects a trap, it'll be pretty obvious from the conversation. He'll be careful about what he says."

Ian gave a curt nod. "You'll be in the next office?"

"We're all set. I don't expect they'll try anything heavy-handed here." The agent's glance slipped briefly toward Katie. He'd insisted she stay at her desk to make the meeting appear normal.

Ian didn't like exposing her to these men again, but she'd argued that the agent was right.

"They don't want to blow a chance to use you," the FBI man pointed out. "Colombian authorities have shut down several of their other operations. The cartel is getting desperate."

When the agent left, it was just Ian and Katie in his office.

"Are you all right with this?" Ian asked.

She nodded, gave him a devil-may-care smile that he guessed was meant to cover her nervousness.

He glanced at the file cabinet. Inside the second drawer was one of the microphones. He didn't want to say anything personal that the men in the next room might pick up, but he felt the need to reassure Katie, as well as himself.

Ian put his arm around her and pulled her close. "I appreciate your supporting me in this, Ms. O'Brien," he said in a proper boss-to-secretary voice.

"I'm happy to cooperate, sir," she responded, just as businesslike, playing along. He felt her body temperature rise by degrees within the curl of his arm.

"If at any time you feel frightened, just get up and leave the room." He kissed her softly, silently on the lips, then whispered in her ear. "Must be the danger, but I'm turned-on. Don't know how I'll be able to leave you alone."

She smiled. "I'll remember that," she said out loud. Then, for the benefit of the men listening from the next room, she repeated, "Get up and leave the room." She kissed him back and shot him a wicked grin that just about left him panting.

"Exactly," he said, running the tip of his finger down her soft throat. Good thing they hadn't also installed cameras. "I would blame myself if an employee of my company was harmed in any way."

"I appreciate your concern, Mr. Danforth." Katie smoothed her hand over the fine silk shirt fabric across his chest, and he drew a sharp breath at her touch. "And now, I'd better go wait in the outer office to greet our visitors. Don't you think?"

He fixed her with an anguished expression before releasing her. "I suppose you should."

Not ten minutes later, the door from the main corridor opened and the two men who had tried to corner Abraham at the gala stepped through. Escalante was in the lead and immediately looked past Katie toward Ian's door. "Mr. Danforth is expecting us."

"Yes, sir." She felt Hernandez studying her, his eyes smoky and hooded. Her flesh crawled under his cold regard. She quickly scooped up her notepad and led the way, knocking on Ian's door before opening it and stepping through.

"Your five-o'clock appointment, sir."

Play the *Lucky Hearts* Game

and get...

2 FREE BOOKS

and a **FREE MYSTERY GIFT...**

yes! YOURS to KEEP!

I have scratched off the silver card.
Please send me my *2 FREE BOOKS* and
FREE mystery GIFT. I understand that I am
under no obligation to purchase any books as
explained on the back of this card.

Scratch Here!
then look below to see
what your cards get you...
2 Free Books & a Free
Mystery Gift!

326 SDL DZ5S   225 SDL DZ57

FIRST NAME

LAST NAME

ADDRESS

APT.#   CITY

STATE/PROV.   ZIP/POSTAL CODE   (S-D-05/04)

Twenty-one gets you
2 FREE BOOKS
and a **FREE MYSTERY GIFT!**

Twenty gets you
2 FREE BOOKS!

Nineteen gets you
1 FREE BOOK!

TRY AGAIN!

Offer limited to one per household and not valid to current Silhouette Desire® subscribers. All orders subject to approval.

© 2004 HARLEQUIN ENTERPRISES LTD.
® and TM are trademarks owned by Harlequin Enterprises Ltd.

◀ DETACH AND MAIL CARD TODAY! ▶

The Silhouette Reader Service™ — Here's how it works:

Accepting your 2 free books and mystery gift places you under no obligation to buy anything. You may keep the books and gift and return the shipping statement marked "cancel." If you do not cancel, about a month later we'll send you 6 additional books and bill you just $3.57 each in the U.S., or $4.24 each in Canada, plus 25¢ shipping & handling per book and applicable taxes if any.* That's the complete price and — compared to cover prices of $4.25 each in the U.S. and $4.99 each in Canada — it's quite a bargain! You may cancel at any time, but if you choose to continue, every month we'll send you 6 more books, which you may either purchase at the discount price or return to us and cancel your subscription.

*Terms and prices subject to change without notice. Sales tax applicable in N.Y. Canadian residents will be charged applicable provincial taxes and GST. Credit or debit balances in a customer's account(s) may be offset by any other outstanding balance owed by or to the customer.

If offer card is missing write to: The Silhouette Reader Service, 3010 Walden Ave., P.O. Box 1867, Buffalo, NY 14240-1867

BUSINESS REPLY MAIL
FIRST-CLASS MAIL   PERMIT NO. 717-003   BUFFALO, NY

POSTAGE WILL BE PAID BY ADDRESSEE

SILHOUETTE READER SERVICE
3010 WALDEN AVE
PO BOX 1867
BUFFALO NY 14240-9952

NO POSTAGE
NECESSARY
IF MAILED
IN THE
UNITED STATES

Ian stood up behind his desk at which he appeared to have been working. "Good. Come in, gentlemen."

They all shook hands then Ian waved them toward chairs strategically placed near microphones.

"We were delighted to hear from you, Mr. Danforth," Escalante said. "It was our understanding that your father had cut off all chances of our working together."

"As was mentioned at the gala, Abraham Danforth has handed over the official reins of this company to me," Ian reminded them. "Although he still has some unofficial say."

"As it should be," Hernandez remarked, his eyes still fixed on Katie. "A man must respect his father."

Katie pulled her chair back a few inches, so that Escalante partially blocked his companion's line of sight.

Ian continued. "I feel my father has been somewhat hasty in turning away your business, Mr. Hernandez. I'm not totally satisfied with the quality of the coffee beans our current supplier has been providing. I might consider changing sources, if what you have to offer is better."

"Our beans are the best Colombia can provide," Hernandez assured him, his attention at last drawn away from Katie.

"But quality of product aside, there are other advantages to dealing with my friend," Escalante added.

"And they are?" Ian turned to the drug lord, his expression intent, controlled, although Katie noticed the dangerous darkening of Ian's eyes.

She held her breath and pretended to take notes.

"We understand," Escalante said, "you've had

some recent trouble here at your corporate headquarters."

The bomb, Katie thought, her heart thudding wildly. *He's talking about the bomb!*

"We have." Ian frowned. "It's very upsetting."

"Particularly with the *señor* planning his political campaign."

"Yes, particularly," Ian echoed, and gave Katie a look, letting her know that he was trying to follow the agents' instructions to let the Colombians do the talking, rather than lead the conversation.

Escalante continued. "So it would be most beneficial if there were no more, let us say…*urgencies?*"

"Of course," Ian responded, an underlying grit and barely restrained fury in his tone. It was clearly costing him to hold his temper, to not throw himself across the desk at these two who were all but bragging to him that they were behind the bomb.

Katie held her tongue but kept her hand moving across the paper, taking down words so carefully chosen that she knew they wouldn't prove anything against the two thugs.

"She have to be here?" Hernandez suddenly asked.

"Ms. O'Brien is my assistant," Ian said. "She sits in on all my meetings. We need a record of our discussion."

Escalante smiled and rested a hand on his partner's arm. "What is wrong with a secretary being here? We are discussing innocent business matters, my friend."

"I know her!" Hernandez snapped.

Katie's blood ran cold. She bit down on her bottom lip and looked helplessly off into the distance. He must have seen the photograph in the *Chronicle.* For several seconds no one spoke.

"Where you know her from?" Escalante asked at last, his voice threatening. "She the law?"

Katie glanced at Ian, who looked puzzled.

"No. She was with him, at that party."

"Of course, she was there." Ian stood up from his desk and faced the two men. "What does that have to do with anything?"

The two Colombians exchanged knowing looks.

"We understand, *señor*. A very practical arrangement." Hernandez smiled smugly at his partner. "Nothing more need be said."

"Back to the matter at hand," Escalante said as Ian took his seat again. "We want to assure you that we take the safety of our business associates seriously. I will personally guarantee you will have no more trouble of the sort you've suffered in the past, if you purchase my associate's coffee beans."

"How can you do that?" Ian asked.

Unless you were the ones who planted that bomb, she finished silently for him. The two men met his demanding gaze, and understanding passed between them. They knew what he was asking, but they didn't fall for the bait.

"We have ways of protecting our interests," Escalante pronounced with a vague wave of his hand. He stood up, and the other two men followed suit. "I believe you understand our position. You know how to reach us, *señor*." He nodded at his associate, and the two turned and left.

Katie shuddered and felt a wave of relief at their departure.

Ian stood without moving behind his desk, looking like a sturdy but storm-shaken oak. He stared at her.

The corridor door closed with a clack, and still neither of them moved.

"That was worthless," he said.

The FBI seconded Ian's assessment of the interview. The Colombians had said nothing that would hold up in any court of law—nothing that could possibly incriminate them for the bombing, or label them as anything but aggressive businessmen trying to land a new account.

Yet the tension of the twenty-minute meeting between Ian and the drug lord and his crony left Katie trembling even after the agents had packed their recording gear and gone.

She sat at her desk, sipping coffee she'd brought up from D&D's. Decaf this time, to soothe her frayed nerves.

"Thanks, Katie."

She looked up to find Ian standing over her. "For what? All I did was make them suspicious because I was here."

"No. Your presence reminded me to keep my mouth shut." He pulled her up out of her chair into his arms and held her tightly. "Dammit, I should have refused to involve you in this. I hated the way those bastards looked at you. It must have been humiliating for you."

"I'm all right," she assured him.

He pulled back to study her face but didn't release her. "You look terrible."

"Flatterer."

He laughed. "Maybe I should insult you more frequently. I could feel the muscles in your back loosen up for a moment."

Katie closed her eyes against the flow of warmth through her body. He was massaging between her shoulder blades and down the silken crevice of her spine. It felt so good.

She sighed and closed her eyes. "Insult me to your heart's content, as long as you keep doing that."

His hands stopped abruptly. "Katie, there's something you have to understand."

"Yes?" She felt languid, floating under the touch of his hands.

"There are very good reasons why you can't work here."

"Let's not talk about that anymore." She sighed. His hands were moving again. Marvelous. Each stroke of his strong fingers seemed to delve deep within her, easing away tension.

"I care about you, Katie. I haven't yet figured out how to deal with that, but I know one thing. I don't want you to get hurt."

She instinctively stiffened at his protective tone. "I'm a big girl. I can take care of myself."

"No doubt, in most cases. But this is getting serious. Just seeing you in the same room with them made me physically ill."

"Ian, really, I was just a little weirded out by the whole situation." She tossed him an irritated look. "I'm okay with it now."

"But I'm not!" he ground out, pushing her none too gently away from him. His eyes were no longer a soft hazel. Blue-gray sparks ignited them. "I worry about you, Katie. What if those creeps tried to get to me through you?"

She laughed. "I'm your assistant. Why would they target a simple employee?"

"No," he shouted, "they realize you were my date at the gala. It's common practice for men in some countries to keep their mistresses conveniently close at hand by giving them a job." He slammed his fist down on the desk, sending a pen flying.

His anger was working on her, driving up her temper to match his. "You're blowing this whole thing out of proportion, Ian." Her throat burned with unshed tears. "Why can't you treat me like any of the other women who work here?"

"Because," he bellowed, "I want to be with you, dammit!"

She stared at him, trying to grasp the meaning behind words that sounded so unromantic when screamed at her.

What was the man really asking for? A relationship meant different things to different people.

She took a deep breath, trying to feel her way along, and spoke quietly. "Obviously, I'm attracted to you, Ian." In truth, she ached for his touch even now, in the midst of their arguing. "But I don't want to get seriously involved with anyone right now. And that's what you're asking me for, isn't it?"

His face flushed, as if she'd slapped him. "But you'd be open to a fling, is that it? An affair that means nothing?"

"That's not what I said!" He was twisting her words, making them sound cheap, and she was furious with him.

The simple fact was, getting involved with Ian Danforth, as in committing herself to a long-term relationship, could only mean trouble. He was a high-profile personality in Savannah. The press kept track of men like that, knew where they dined, and with whom.

As far as she knew, she'd successfully avoided photographers at the gala. If a reporter found out they were a couple, her photo would suddenly pop up in a dozen society columns across the country. She still wasn't sure that Jasmine hadn't recognized her.

"I just don't want a man thinking I'm his possession," she tried to justify herself, which was part of the truth.

He shook his head, staring in disbelief at her. "I'm not like that, Katie." Ian reached out and took her arm, pulling her back toward him. "Give us a chance to get to know each other better."

She shook him free and stepped away, staring at the floor, unable to meet his eyes. She desperately wanted to tell him the truth, ached to fall into his arms and let him make all the decisions. But if she did that, her newly found freedom would be lost.

"I've been smothered by caring people all of my life," she murmured. "I've had enough."

She spun away from him, dashing for the door. He didn't try to stop her this time.

The lump in her throat made it impossible for her to swallow. Salty tears, coming in great sobs, racked her body. All brave talk, she thought wildly, hopelessly. But in her heart, she didn't want to leave Ian. She needed his touch, longed for his strong arms. It was just that there were too many strings attached to being his lover.

Katie stopped with her hand on the doorknob, overwhelmed by sadness, letting the tears fall.

"You know," she whispered, "if any man ever just let me be myself, I might fall in love with him."

She flung open the door and started through it, but

strong hands seized her from behind and pulled her back into the office. Into his arms.

"Dammit, Katie, you confuse the hell out of me!" Ian shook his head violently, as if words didn't suffice for emotions so strong. His lips covered hers. He held her fiercely to his chest.

Katie clutched fistfuls of his suit jacket, tugging until it slid off his shoulders. He shrugged out of it. She pulled out his shirttail and slipped her hands up under the crisp fabric to feel the warm, crinkly mat of chest hairs and underlying muscles.

Ian moaned between her lips and began undressing her. She felt her skirt descend over her hips and fall to her ankles. His hands smoothed over her hips, tucked beneath the sheer silk of her panties, and cupped her bottom, pressing her up and into his hardness.

She felt herself go liquid, hot and tickly inside.

It had been a long time since she'd slept with a man. The two lovers she'd ever had were hardly more than boys.

Ian was no boy.

He lifted her off her feet and easily carried her across the room. Not for a moment did he stop kissing her, and she could only guess that they were headed for the leather couch at the far end of his office. He placed her on it and immediately stretched out on top of her. The heat of his body seared through her remaining clothing, her blouse, bra and panties.

All concerns for her independence melted away. If, moments earlier, being with Ian had seemed threatening for any reason, now she couldn't imagine not being here, like this, with him.

Katie raked her fingers through the fine, short hairs

up the back of his neck, and pressed his head closer, making his kiss harder against her mouth. She felt alive. Dizzy with feminine power and passion so thick she imagined scooping it up with a spoon and relishing it as she would a rich dessert.

The ridge of his erection—so very hard and long—told her that he must want her very badly. She opened her mouth to ask if he had protection when the sound of a door opening and closing intruded on her rapture.

Ian's body tightened on top of her, his breathing thin and rapid in her ear.

"Who is it?" he called toward the outer office.

"Ian, you in there?"

"Who?" Katie asked hoarsely.

"My brother, Reid!"

He pushed up off her. In two strides he reached the door and turned the button lock in the knob. A heartbeat later, the knob jiggled.

Katie sat up, hurriedly buttoning her blouse. She cast Ian a look of pure panic but didn't dare say anything.

"Hold on, Reid," he called through the door. "I'll be right out."

"Yeah, sure," a puzzled voice came back, followed by a laugh. "What's with the lock? You got a hot babe in there with you, big brother?"

"Of course." Ian winked at Katie. "Just like any other workday."

"Stop that!" she hissed, stooping to pluck skirt and shoes from the floor.

Ian grinned and handed her a tangled mass of panty hose. "Hey, it's okay," he whispered. "I'll get rid of him. Sit tight." He unlocked the door while Katie stood with her clothing clutched to her chest. He slipped through as narrow a crack as possible into the outer office.

Katie gasped for breath and pulled on her skirt, trying to manage the button on the waistband with trembling fingers.

Was the man mad?

More to the point, had she lost her own mind? What was she doing sprawling half-naked on her boss's couch? Rebelling against her parents? Or had she simply lost the ability to behave rationally?

Hastily she finished dressing then let herself out of his office through a side door that connected to the fifth-floor conference room. She could hear Ian and his brother on the other side of the common wall. They were laughing.

The exact source of their humor, she could too easily guess. But wasn't that, in a way, her own fault? Hadn't she told Ian she wasn't looking for anything serious? And men just naturally interpreted a statement like that to suit their own needs.

As he'd said…a fling…an affair.

Her head pounded and her throat felt raw with tears she had no time to shed.

Katie peeked through the conference-room door that led directly into the corridor. The coast was clear. She ran for the rear stairwell and shot down five flights to the street in no time at all. Not until she reached her apartment building did she stop running, and then it was to buzz a neighbor, asking to be let in. Because her purse with her keys was still sitting in her desk. And no way was she going back for it tonight.

Seven

Ian looked up from the investment prospectus his cousin Imogene had given him to study before they met that morning. Unfortunately, his mind wasn't on business.

He glanced at the clock on his desk: 8:45 a.m. Katie was late. After their rushed parting the night before, he wasn't even sure she'd turn up today. He'd tried to call her last night, but she hadn't picked up her phone.

He closed his eyes and swore at himself, at Katie…at the female sex in general. Relationships were so damn complicated. And Katie was just about the easiest woman in the world to spook. She was keeping secrets, but whatever might be haunting her, she wasn't telling.

He wondered why she wouldn't confide in him. What could be so terrible that she didn't dare share the truth with him? Just considering the possibilities tore him up inside. Dammit. He had the power to help her—money and influence to protect her if she was in trouble.

The metallic sound of file-cabinet drawers opening and closing in the outer office snapped him out of his gray funk.

Ian launched himself at his door, swung it open.

Katie jumped back from an open drawer. "Jeez, don't do that! You scared me to death, popping out like a big jack-in-the-box."

He scowled at her and all his carefully prepared tactfulness flew out the window. "Where the hell did you go yesterday?"

"Home," she replied, flipping through files with great purpose.

"Why?"

"Wasn't that obvious?" She slanted him a withering look. "You and your brother were having a good male chuckle over our tussle on your couch. As the object of your humor, I chose not to hang around."

"We weren't laughing at you," he groaned. "In fact, I was being discreet in trying to get him to leave. But he was all jazzed up about a joke he'd heard from one of the sales reps. I couldn't get him to leave until he'd told it."

"Right," she said.

"It's the truth! If you'd stayed another five minutes, we'd have been alone and…" He moved in closer, touched her gently at the waist. "We could have finished what we started."

She stiffened, although her eyes took on a smoky haze. He was reassured; she wasn't immune to him. "I had second thoughts," she murmured. "It's just not possible, Ian."

''Why the hell not? You acted as if anything was possible before Reid showed up.''

She started to turn away but he stepped around her, forcing her to face him. ''You know I wouldn't hurt you, Katie. What are you so afraid of?''

''Nothing.'' She refused to meet his eyes.

''No,'' he insisted, ''it's something important. You go out of your way to avoid connecting with me on any level but professionally, except that every once in a while you slip. Your heart steps in, overrides your head, and your body begins to talk to me.''

''That's ridiculous.''

''Is it? What about yesterday on the couch? Are you going to claim I seduced you, or forced you?''

''Of course not.''

''Then how did that happen if you aren't interested in being with me? And what was that crack about falling in love, if you don't want to get serious about a relationship?''

''Don't shout,'' she said, sounding frustrated and close to tears.

''I'm not shouting!'' he shouted, then winced at the harshness of his own voice. ''I'm trying to make a point,'' he said, making the words softer. ''You send me mixed signals, Katie, one minute to the next. You want to be with me, but you seem terrified of being seen with me in public. I know next to nothing about you. Who are you and what is this all about?''

''I'm nobody,'' she sobbed. ''I just want to figure out who I'm supposed to be, find out what I'm good at and be on my own for a while. Is that too much to ask?''

He frowned at her. ''I respect your goals. They're all worthy.'' He thought for a moment. ''Do you realize, when I first met you, you seemed the most self-assured young woman I'd ever met. You blew in here, a veritable tornado of energy, and took over everything—me, the office decor, the business of the day.''

"I did, didn't I?" She smiled weakly.

"Yes. You also took my breath away with those saucy green eyes and that tumble of red curls and—" he let his eyes drop the length of her body "—the rest of the package. You made me want to try again. You made me want to take risks.''

She blushed and blinked up at him but said nothing.

"Listen," he went on, "I respect your right to experiment, to discover yourself, if that's what you think you need to do. But I don't understand why you can't let me into your life while you're doing it. And I wish, just once, you'd give me a straight answer to one simple question. Who has frightened you so badly?''

She sniffled and swiped at tears drying on her cheeks. "I honestly can't tell you.''

"Do you think I'd give you away? Don't you trust me?''

"I do, Ian." Her eyes were the deepest, loveliest emerald, all the brighter for her tears. And they broke his heart. "It's just that…that you might not see things my way. If you sided with *them,* you'd feel compelled to do something. I'm not ready to face that moment yet." She laid a hand on his. "Please. Give me time to work things out my way.''

He stared at her, then shook his head and walked back into his office. He shut the door behind him, putting up a physical barrier in addition to the emotional barricade she'd erected between them.

To hell with work, he thought. It just wasn't going to happen.

* * *

Katie walked into D&D's on the first floor, craving her morning cappuccino break. She drew up short at the sight of Ian seated at a table near the counter with Imogene Danforth. She hadn't realized, when the two had left the office half an hour earlier, that they'd be meeting here, on what she'd come to think of as her turf. She often came to D&D's on breaks to relax in the cozy coffee shop with other employees.

She tried to pass by them unnoticed, but Ian spotted her and waved her over.

Imogene handed Ian an annotated prospectus they'd obviously been reviewing together and snapped shut her valise. "Well, that's about it. I recommend that portfolio of bonds as a hedge against the current volatile stock market. It's a sound investment for Danforth's."

"Looks good to me. Thanks, Imogene," Ian said.

"Great, so we'll go ahead with the agreed-upon purchase?"

Ian nodded.

Imogene glanced vaguely in Katie's direction, standing behind Ian's chair. "Can you run upstairs and photocopy these documents for us, dear?" She didn't even meet Katie's eyes as she shoved papers into her hands. "Fax me copies this afternoon."

Imogene checked her gold designer watch then turned back to Ian. "I have another appointment in fifteen minutes. Gotta run, cuz." She pecked him on the cheek. "Wish Abraham good luck for me. I understand he's off again campaigning."

Ian nodded. "The man has more energy than I do."

Imogene let out an appreciative laugh but was already halfway out the door.

"I'll go do this right away," Katie murmured.

She didn't appreciate being treated like the hired help. Her Fortune pride rebelled. But, she rationalized, this was her job and she had no real grounds for complaint. Except, if she were in Imogene's executive shoes she would at least say please when asking employees for a favor, and give them a smile of thanks.

Still, in a way, she admired Imogene. She was an independent woman with a great career as an investment broker, an air of self-possession and super clothes. She mentally calculated how many paychecks it would take a lowly clerk like her to afford such a smashing silk suit.

"Wait!" Ian barked.

Katie swiveled round to see him still seated at the table. She felt nauseous at the thought of deceiving him any longer. Very soon she would have to straighten out her identity.

The real Katie O'Brien would eventually move back to Savannah. Holly had her real Social Security number; Katherine knew enough about the law to realize she could get into real trouble by falsifying income and tax records. It was only a matter of time before Holly, overwhelmed with work lately, caught the mismatch between the social security number on her application and her adopted name.

Slowly Katie walked back to the table and Ian.

"Listen," he said, pulling out the chair beside him for her. "I need to apologize."

"No, you don't. With what your family and company has been dealing with you have to be careful. I've been behaving in ways you can't possibly understand, and it worries you." She shrugged then looked directly up into his dark eyes. "Please believe me, Ian, my problems have nothing to do with the Danforths. I'm not a danger to your company or your father's campaign, if that's what you're thinking."

"I'm mostly thinking about you. If you're in trouble—"

She held up a hand to stop him from going on, but he ignored her.

"I want to help," he said firmly. "Let me."

She shook her head. "It's my problem. I have to deal with it."

He reached over and took her hand. Despite her resolve to keep an emotional distance from him, his touch was comforting. "Don't run away from the truth. If it scares you, facing it down is the only way. No matter how bad it might seem."

She laughed. "You sound as if you think I'm some kind of criminal on the lam."

He quirked a dark brow at her. "Are you?"

"Not even close." She sighed, aching to tell him but knowing he'd disapprove. After all, he was close to his own family. He thrived within the Danforth clan's circle of business and social contacts. He'd never understand someone who saw her own family as the enemy. "Listen, I need to get back to the office. I have a ton of work." She smiled mischievously. "And a tyrant for a boss."

He grinned at her. "Is that what the hired help thinks of me?"

She tossed her head, sending vibrant curls flying. "Actually, if you heard the gossip around the watercooler, you'd blush." She eyed him speculatively. "Maybe not. Maybe you'd just get a swelled head." She leaned toward him as she stood up from the table, and whispered, "You're on the single woman's most-wanted list."

He blinked in surprise, then laughed out loud and stood up to follow her from the shop. She walked quickly across the lobby with Ian striding to keep up with her.

"All right," he said as they waited for the elevator, "just promise me if you're ever desperate and change your mind about wanting help, you'll come to me."

"I will," she agreed, and stepped into the elevator car.

Just then, a movement across the crowded lobby caught her eye. A set of wide shoulders. A flicker of a familiar profile. She stared at the man in western-style suit, just as he turned and focused on her face through the narrowing space between the slowly closing elevator doors.

For a breathless moment, her heart raced. Her knees went numb, wobbly.

Katie gave an involuntary gasp. "No!"

"What?" Ian demanded, staring at her with concern.

She couldn't answer, couldn't breathe. Her chest ached and she looked around wildly, feeling trapped.

The man in the lobby pushed between people, rushing toward the elevator, shouting for it to stop. Just before the doors sighed shut, he lunged for them, his face screwed up in a mask of urgency.

Katie fell back against other passengers. Horrified, she heard what she imagined were the man's fists pounding on the outer doors as the car started to climb. Passengers behind her whispered nervously.

"Talk about being in a hurry," one man mumbled, and got a laugh.

Katie didn't dare look at Ian, but she felt him watching her and knew a storm was brewing. Doesn't matter, she told herself, she had more to worry about than a confused boss at the moment.

As soon as the doors opened wide enough to let her through to the fifth floor, she shot between them, her mind whirring.

Ian ran behind her. "Who was that man?"

She couldn't speak, couldn't even fathom what to do next. They'd found her! Her brother Dennis had somehow traced her to Savannah. Oh God, what now?

"Katie, talk to me. Please!" Ian grabbed her arm, but she slipped from his fingers. "Is that man harassing you? We'll call the police!"

"Don't. Please don't. I'm all right. Really, I am." Ian would only make things worse if she involved him now. He couldn't possibly understand. She was running down the hall, tossing words over her shoulder at him. "I can't stay. I have to... I'll be back. Just let me sort things out."

She might still get out of the building and back to her apartment without Dennis catching up with her. She could think things through in peace there.

"Katie!" Ian's plea crested over her like a warm wave, beckoning to her.

She didn't slow down.

It tore Ian apart.

Katie was running from a man, and Ian didn't want another man in her life. He didn't care if that was selfish.

If she was still this emotionally tied to the handsome young fellow in the Stetson he'd glimpsed in the lobby, maybe she still loved him. Maybe she would go back to him. Then Ian would never know what it was to love her. Really love her.

For the first time he was able to acknowledge why they bickered over even the most insignificant things in the office. He was like the kindergarten kid who picks on one little girl in his class because he likes her. He had been tugging Katie's pigtails, figuratively speaking, since her first day at Danforth's. He had annoyed her and fought with her, and he'd even tried to get her removed from his office. When none of that worked, he did what he'd really wanted to do all along. Make love to her.

The male mind is truly perverse, he thought to himself.

That afternoon Ian called her apartment three times. Either she wasn't there or wasn't answering.

Maybe she was so terrified of that man she'd been afraid to go home. Before he left the office for the day, he scanned the lobby and the coffee shop, just to see if he could spot the man again. If he did, he'd sure as hell confront him and demand to know his reason for stalking Katie. But the man in the Stetson was nowhere to be seen.

That night, Ian nearly went mad with worry. He telephoned her place three more times, leaving messages for her to call him. A dozen times, he nearly rang up the police. Each time, he reminded himself that she'd begged him to trust her. If he broke that trust to follow his own instincts, she might hate him for it.

An infinitesimally fine thread bound them now. He dared not strain it.

Hadn't she said more than once that she needed to learn to be on her own, discover her strengths? Maybe

she viewed this as a personal test. If he failed to respect her wishes, his interference might turn her totally
against him.

So he waited through the long night, drank way too
much bourbon and hoped he was doing the right thing.

Ian picked up two cups of D&D's best on his way
up to the office the next morning. Just habit, he realized after he had the coffee in hand. There was no
guarantee Katie would appear, given what had happened the day before.

But when he walked into the CEO's suite, juggling
steaming cups to manage the doorknob, she sat at her
desk, looking pale and exhausted but composed.

She looked up at him, then saw the coffee. "Oh,
yes, yes, yes! Thank you so much," she said softly.
"Wonderful caffeine. We were out of our office supply." She snatched the cup from him and took a grateful, long drink.

He hesitated, unsure what to say without prying or
treading on ground she protected so tenaciously. "Is
everything all right?" he asked cautiously.

"It will be." She smiled tentatively at him and pried
the plastic lid off her cup to savor an even longer
creamy guzzle. "We'll talk soon. About everything, I
promise. I just have to make sense of some things in
my own head before I try to explain them to anyone
else."

He nodded. "I'm here when you're ready, Katie."

She gave him a slightly brighter smile. "Thanks."

He walked into his office, quietly shut the door behind him and let out a string of curses. The act of
relinquishing control to someone else was nearly the
toughest thing he'd ever done. It was his nature to

never stand by and let someone close to him suffer. And although Katie was putting up a good front, he was sure she was suffering.

That was what had been so difficult about losing his unborn child. He had been helpless to stop it from happening. He felt no less helpless now.

All that day and the next, Katie felt as if she were holding her breath. Her brother might open the door to Ian's office and walk in at any moment, but she couldn't just hide in the apartment, waiting for him to leave Savannah.

Katie decided that, come what may, she had to live her life. Furthermore, as she began to think more clearly about the incident, she realized that it was possible Dennis had simply wandered into the building as he searched the city. It might have been pure luck that they'd ended up in the same place at the same time.

And what if he did check with Personnel? He'd ask for Katherine Fortune, a name that wouldn't come up on their records. He had no way of connecting her with the real or fictional Katie O'Brien. Katie had been one of many friends from college; she'd never come home with her to meet the family. Just to be safe, though, she took the precaution of using the back stairway as she came and went. After a couple more days passed, she'd feel confident she'd shaken Dennis.

All she asked for was a little more time. Once she was assured of a permanent position with Danforth's she'd have bargaining power. Then she could say to her parents, "See, I've made a life for myself. I'm gainfully employed, supporting myself, and I'm happy here." Her father would have to acknowledge her right to independence then, wouldn't he?

Two more days passed, and her worry over her brother lessened. However the tension she felt emanating from Ian increased. He kept his distance, maybe just to give her space…maybe rethinking his interest in her. She vowed that the very next day she would explain everything to him. She would do it carefully, to lessen the impact of her lying to him. She would say the right things to help him understand her point of view. It wasn't that she hated her family or felt they didn't have a right to know she was safe. She simply needed to be her own person, and that was hard to do if you were a Fortune woman.

Meanwhile she missed having his arms around her. She hoped that after he knew the truth, he would still want her.

Ian slapped shut the updated portfolio Imogene had left with him. None of the figures made sense; they buzzed in his head like angry bees.

Something had to give.

He reached for the call button on his phone to summon Katie, then changed his mind. When he walked out into the reception area, she was seated at her desk, staring at the screen saver on her PC.

"Katie."

She jumped.

"Don't worry," he said quickly, "no grand inquisition."

She turned and looked up at him from her chair. He rested his hands on her shoulders and gazed down at her. Her eyes grew bright, her cheeks flushed, but she held his gaze. He would give anything to be able to haul her up into his arms and keep her there.

"It's getting late," he said. "You should have left over an hour ago."

She lifted a shoulder under his hand. "It's okay. There's work to be done. I don't have anywhere special to go."

Was she waiting for dark to leave the building? Was she still running?

"I want to kiss you." The words were out before he had time to censor the thought that had triggered them.

She tilted her head and observed his face, as deeply contemplative and innocent as a child studying a daisy. "I would like that very much."

She stood up and melted against him. He felt as if the universe had suddenly shrunk to the size of the one square foot where they stood. Her lips parted invitingly and he was lost.

Ian kissed her the way he'd dreamed of kissing her ever since they'd met. He possessed her mouth, caressed the small of her back, pressed her closer still to his body. When he at last drew his head back to breathe, her eyes grew instantly wary.

"No questions asked," he promised. "No grilling under a hot light, no demands. You make all the calls, Katie."

A look of amazement and relief crossed her face. "Really?"

"If that's the only way I can have you, that's what I'll take."

Katie felt the world lift from her shoulders. Never had a man told her that he would follow her lead. Not in love. Not in family life. Not in school or business. Yet Ian, who was so accustomed to being in charge, had relinquished control to her, had blindly accepted her despite all the risks he must have perceived.

He'd been terribly hurt before, she knew that much. He'd had a wife and, nearly, a child…and lost both. Now he was taking what she imagined must be an immense leap of faith for him. More than anything, she didn't want to disappoint him.

Tonight they would make love. Tomorrow she would tell him who she was, why she was hiding from her family, and hope that he could understand how important it was to her.

Right now, she wanted a lover. A grown-up, experienced, exciting lover.

Ian's arm felt strong and warm around her waist as he led her to the leather couch in his office. They sat down together. Although she sensed a catlike, predatory tension in his body as he drew her into his arms, and his eyes revealed a hunger she hoped she could satisfy, he reined in his wilder impulses.

Gently he brushed his lips across hers, moved his hands over her body, through her clothing. It was nice.

But nice wasn't what she wanted. Her own needs, her own hungers were clawing at her, demanding more…wanting him to move faster. She needed hard. She needed intense. Burning and wicked and wanton. No sweet schoolboy kisses or experimental touches for her.

Her excitement built in equal proportion to her frustration. At last Katie pulled away from Ian's tender embrace and stared him dead in the eyes.

"No," she said.

He looked startled, then disappointed. "I'm sorry, I thought you wanted to make love."

"Ian, I'm not a child. I'm younger than you, yes,

but you're not doing anything wrong by having sex with me.''

He frowned. ''I just don't want to hurt you. Maybe we should go to my place. It's more appropriate.''

''I'm not a piece of Spode china. I won't break. And I don't want a change of venue. I want you...*now*...*here*.'' She punctuated each word with a tug at his belt buckle until it fell open.

One dark brow lifted. ''You know about this not breaking business from vast past experience?'' He sounded more than a little worried.

She laughed. ''I've had boyfriends before, not a football squad.''

''Well, that's a relief.''

She yanked him down on top of her, wedged one knee between his thighs and nudged him. ''I want passion, Mr. Danforth.''

''Passion.'' His voice sounded hoarse.

''Do what you feel like doing, not what you think is proper. I've had proper all of my life. It's gotten damn old.''

It was as if she'd thrown an electrical switch on the man. Not one of those puny wall switches that make an ordinary ceiling light flicker on. This was the lever type she imagined a groundskeeper yanking down to set a major-league stadium ablaze in the night.

With one hand on either side of her hips, he slid her down on the leather cushions, leaving her skirt in folds around her waist. She could feel his erection through the tissue-thin lining of her panties, rigid and hard against the tender flesh between her thighs.

Had he been this aroused moments ago? Had he somehow managed to disguise his lust because he'd thought he should?

Impressive self-control, the thought came to her through a hot, sensual haze. She was throbbing down there, and wondered if he could feel that deep, resonant feminine pulse.

Then, in a heartbeat, the mere act of thinking was impossible. His mouth covered hers. She parted her lips in a gasp of pleasure as his tongue probed, demanded. His hands were loosening her clothing, dispensing quickly with blouse, bra, until she was naked from the waist up. Her breasts rubbed against the coarse linen of his jacket. The little white pearl buttons of his shirtfront lightly scraped against her nipples, sending licks of heat to heighten the blaze within her.

Frantically she attempted to unbutton his shirt, needing to touch his flesh. But he brushed her hands aside. "No," he growled. "Like this. I want you like this."

She, unclothed, provocative. He, urbanely dressed, her master.

Did she mind? Not in the least.

Relinquishing her body to him, giving him permission to take control of their pleasure…it felt right. She'd given herself over to him freely.

Already the intensity of his lovemaking had opened new vistas of sensation. It was as if she could glimpse distant horizons she'd never seen before, feel deeper pleasure and pain than her body had been capable of until this moment. The room glimmered around them—all brass and polished mahogany and butter-soft leather. And his eyes were oh so dark above her. Every inch of him, though clothed and kept from her fingertips itching to explore, was taut with pent-up desire primed to engulf her.

"Sorry. Buy you new ones," he growled in her ear,

which made no sense at all, until she felt her panties come away in shreds at a tug of his fingers.

Thrilled by his strength, she closed her eyes and let her head fall back against his supporting hand. His breath fell hot along her throat, across her breasts. He drew his tongue in lazy circles round one nipple then the other before falling with a throaty male groan over the easiest to reach, drawing her breast succulently, eagerly into his mouth.

She delighted at the sensation of his teeth, his tongue, as they savored her. Tender flesh quivered and prickled deliciously with each sweep of his tongue and lips.

"Oh!" she gasped. "Please, don't stop." She pressed his head down harder and felt herself grow wet with ecstasy.

Ian cupped her bare bottom, moved her thighs apart and rubbed her against the coarse linen of his pants front, until she begged him again and again to take her. Her body ripened, gave way, flowed hot and steady. She moaned.

He didn't ask if she was all right with what he was doing to her. It was as if he understood what each shiver, each subtle twitch of muscle and unlocked emotion meant. He seemed to sense, too, where and when to touch her, and just how tenderly or vigorously to create the most intense reactions in her body. She wondered, fleetingly, how on earth he was managing to control himself, for he'd been fully ready for what seemed a very long time. Pleasuring her…only her.

"Ian!" she cried out as he slipped a hand between their bodies and touched for the first time the sex-plumped flesh between her thighs.

"Yes, my love," he whispered.

"I didn't know...didn't think..." It hadn't been like this before. Ever.

"Don't think," he cautioned, "only feel."

"But—"

His lips covered hers, shutting off words she couldn't have found anyway. His fingertips sought out her sensitive, moist core, plunged within her in quick, eager thrusts, and she arched her back and rocked against his hand until the exploding waves of heat subsided within her as smoldering embers.

"Please," she begged, weakly, "let me touch you."

He smiled tightly. "Can't, love."

"Why? I want to wrap my fingers around you and...oh, Ian, please!"

"No. When I come I'm going to be in you. Touch me now, and it's a done deal." His eyes glowed darkly—a shadow of the predator again. The tiger standing over his prey. Any moment and he'd devour her.

Then, as if he suddenly saw his limit, he reached for his zipper. Looking down she watched as he hastily freed himself from pants and briefs without removing either.

She couldn't take her eyes off his generous, perfectly formed shaft—so hard, so satisfyingly full and long. He plucked a small foil square from his pocket and, as she admired him, he protected them.

Katie felt an inner twinge at the reality of the moment. Now came the promise of fulfillment. Now she would be his, and he her very own.

Then, without any effort from her, he was reversing their positions, lifting and settling her astride his slim hips as he lay back along the couch. He spread her, slid her down over him, and every inch of silken shaft brought sleeping nerves to life as he plunged deeper, deeper still within her.

What had once been empty was full. What had once been incomplete was perfect in its completion. Now it seemed only natural that she should be drenched anew and quivering around him.

Ian lifted and lowered her again and again as her fingers curled into the working muscles of his shoulders for support. She imagined she cried out his name but couldn't be sure. A vision of a cave in the Arizona desert appeared to her. The place where lovers' souls melded. This office was their cave. Their place to become one.

Eight

Ian rolled to his side, wrapping himself around Katie on the couch, sheltering her nakedness with his half-clothed body as the final pulses of masculine release and deep pleasure consumed him. The intensity of such an experience, he warned himself, would never be duplicated. What he'd just felt with her was unique, though impossible to describe.

How could a man come away feeling vanquished after ravishing a woman? Yet that was how it seemed. As aggressively as he'd taken her, he was the one left shaken to his very core.

Ian eased his hips back, withdrawing from her, then aligned his body with hers on the generous cushions. He cradled her against him, her long bare legs looping over the couch arm, her head pillowed on his chest. His chin settled into the auburn curls as he stroked her, calming her until the afterquakes of her climaxes subsided.

He was so moved by her hunger for him, by his own response, he couldn't find his voice for the longest time.

When he was sure he'd regained a near-normal ability to speak, he whispered into her ear, "That's why we can't work together."

Katie let out a low throaty laugh. "You win. How about separate offices?"

"On different floors…but even then." He kissed the top of her head. "I'd come prowling for you."

"We could go to your place or mine for lunch every day."

He choked on a laugh. What did the woman think he was made of? "I'd die of exhaustion within a week."

"We don't want that." He felt the muscles of her cheek twitch into a smile, as if she, too, was pleased by his delight in her.

"Not that I wouldn't thoroughly enjoy lunch in bed with you every day." He tried to find a rational way of fitting what had just happened between them into the rest of his well-ordered life. "There's just so much happening now that I have to take care of. Business comes first."

She sat upright as she reached for her blouse on the floor and began pulling it on, although her bra remained looped over the back of a chair. "I see. Business." Her tone was brisk, hurt.

"Katie." He turned her to face him. "I'm not brushing you off. This isn't a one-time thing. I want you in my life. Do you understand?"

"How in your life?" she asked warily.

He sighed. "If tonight is any indication…" He released her, suddenly confused. How much of what he was feeling now was her magic, the lingering passion that clouded a man's mind and made him promise more than he could deliver? "Maybe this discussion should wait. I have a lot to figure out, and you still have issues to sort through." What they were, he still had no clue.

"True," she agreed, but couldn't seem to meet his questioning eyes.

His gut knotted. He retrieved her bra for her, and she held it in her lap as if she'd forgotten where it belonged.

"Don't worry," he said quickly, "I'm not asking for explanations you're not ready to give just because we've become lovers. But I do want to help you any way I can. And I want you in my arms however often we can manage." He took a deep breath. "Just don't walk out of my life because you're frightened of something. Whatever it is, we'll deal with it." He hated her silence, the thoughtful pout of her lips. "Agreed?"

"Yes." Her eyes regained some of their sparkle. She kissed him lightly on the cheek.

"Come on, get dressed." He stood up to tuck in his shirt and buckle his belt. "I'll give you a lift home."

She smiled at him as she headed for the outer office. He followed, watching her drop her bra and shredded panties into her purse. A devilish lick of lust set him wondering if he was already capable of another—

She touched his arm, interrupting his thoughts. "Ian, if you don't mind, I'd rather walk home."

"Alone?" He was disappointed, then concerned. "It's late."

"I know. But the historic quarter is perfectly safe,

and I need time to do some thinking. Really, I'll be fine.''

''If you're sure,'' he said. But he felt compelled to take her in his arms one last time, and after a sweet, lingering kiss, he let her go.

Ian stood alone beside her desk, thinking of her as he heard her steps fade down the corridor, smelling her on his shirt. After a while he began going through the mindless routine of shutting off the office equipment, locking away important files, turning out lights.

The drapes in his office, luckily, had been drawn across the smoky sweep of glass overlooking the city while they made love. At that thought, another trickle of lust. She, spread out naked along beige leather. He, coming down over her.

He closed his eyes to better hold on to the image. It slowly faded, but not without leaving him wanting her, eager for the next time they'd be together like this. And there would be a next time, he promised himself.

But for now he let go of the thought and routine took over. He liked to come into his office in the morning to see the sun slanting through the windows, so he went to them now to open the heavy draperies.

As if he knew she'd be there, he looked down to the street. Katie stepped out from the front entrance of the Danforth Building into a shaft of light from a streetlamp.

He smiled, feeling as good as he'd ever felt. Better! At one time he'd believed he would never find a woman to fill his emptiness, to chase away the ultimate loss of his child's life.

Was it possible he'd been fortunate enough to find the ideal woman to teach him to feel joy again? To heal him and give him hope?

He started to turn away from the window when, from the shadowed alley that ran beside the building, a figure stepped out in front of Katie. Ian's heart stopped. His mouth went sand-dune dry. He stared down five stories as she spoke to the man. Someone she knew?

Then, as Ian watched in horror, the stranger grasped her arm and started pulling her toward a car parked at the curb.

With a curse and a surge of adrenaline, he spun away from the windows and raced for the elevator. His heart hammered within his chest as he dove into the elevator, punched the lobby button. Interminable seconds later he was racing through the empty lobby, bursting between glass doors into the street. He ran toward the two figures struggling on the sidewalk.

"Get away from her, you bastard!" he shouted.

From the little he could see in the dark as he closed in on them, Katie's attacker seemed to be the same man who had sent her in a panicked run the other day. He wore a Stetson, western boots, and had Katie by the wrist.

She dug in her heels, trying to resist his progress toward the car.

In the split second before Ian rammed into the guy's gut with his shoulder, the man looked up with an expression of shock and dismay. The next moment they were both flat on the pavement, scrambling and swinging at each other. Ian rolled just far enough away to get to his knees, seize the man by the knot in his string tie and punch him in the face.

From somewhere in the background came a strange wailing sound. Then fists were pounding on his back.

"Don't, Ian! Oh, God, don't hurt him. Stop, stop it now!"

Confused and distracted by her pleas on behalf of her assailant, Ian didn't see the left hook coming. Knuckles like steel ball bearings smashed into his jaw, set his head spinning. He came back with a fist to the guy's gut, which resulted in a low moan as the man collapsed onto the sidewalk, gasping for breath.

"Go call the police!" Ian shouted over his shoulder at Katie, who was still, inexplicably, pummeling him and sobbing for him to stop. He staggered to his feet. "What?"

"Ian," she choked out, "please don't kill my brother."

He stared at her. "Brother?"

She nodded meekly. "Meet my brother Dennis. Dennis," she added politely to the man still sprawled on the sidewalk, "this is my boss, Ian Danforth."

It took a while for her words to make any sense. Ian glared at the young man who had managed to make it as far as his knees though he was still fighting for breath. When the fellow looked up at Ian with eyes as vividly green as Katie's, a trickle of blood escaping a split lip, Ian swore and held out a hand to help him to his feet.

"I thought you were being kidnapped!" Ian growled at Katie.

"Well, I was. In a way." She shook her mussed hair out of her eyes. "Dennis tends to take my parents' requests a bit too literally." She made a face at her brother. "When they told you to drag me back home, I don't think this was what they had in mind, Den."

The two men faced each other. Neither was smiling or offered a hand to shake.

"Care to further explain the little drama I witnessed from my office window?" Ian asked, brushing grit from the knees of his pants.

Katie stared at the sidewalk, looking dismal.

Dennis touched fingers to his lip and winced. "I was trying to convince my sister to come back to Arizona, that's all."

"You were forcing me into the damn car!" she shot back. "You have no right! None at all—"

"Mom and Dad have been worried sick about you!"

"That doesn't give you the right to—"

"—to do what's best for you?" Dennis interrupted angrily.

"The right to run my life!" Katie was in tears now. Fists on her hips, she stomped her foot at him. "It's not fair. I've never been allowed to do what I want to do. Never—"

Her brother's expression softened. "Katherine, it's only because they care."

"Katherine?" Ian stepped forward.

They both looked at him—Katie with terror in her pretty eyes, Dennis with suspicion.

"Katherine Fortune," the younger man said. "That's her name. If you're her boss, you'd know that."

"I *am* her boss. But that's not the name I know her by." He turned to her looking shocked and angry. "You're the missing heiress?"

Katie winced as if she'd been slapped. "I guess I should explain a few things."

"I guess you should," Ian agreed.

Katie led the way back into the CEO's suite, her stomach tied in a knot as big as the state of Georgia. This was her worst nightmare come true.

It had been bad enough, the anticipation of having to tell Ian she'd deceived him. But at least if it had happened as she'd planned, perhaps over a cozy dinner for two, the news would have come from her. Calmly. Rationally.

She'd have found a way to make him understand why she'd left home. Why she'd used her friend's name to secure a job and start a new life on her own.

But this? She felt sick to her stomach. This was bad. The truth coming from her brother, in the middle of the night. Two men brawling on the street. She dared not consider what Ian thought of her.

Like a condemned prisoner, Katie walked straight through the reception area and into Ian's office. She dropped into the first chair she came to. She lowered her face into her hands and wept.

A moment later someone sat down on the arm of the chair and put a hand on her shoulder. When she peeked between her fingers, she was surprised to find it was Ian.

"Suppose, Katie…Katherine, you explain the situation a little more clearly."

"What's to explain!" Dennis ranted, a handkerchief pressed to his torn lip. "She ran away from home without a word of explanation to anyone. Nothing to indicate where she'd gone. No phone number. No address in case we needed to reach her."

"Right!" she huffed at him. "Like, that's what people do when they escape from their smothering families. Leave a forwarding address."

"Think of Mom and Dad, Katherine! It would have saved them a ton of grief if you'd at least let someone know you were all right."

"I left a note in my room." She sighed. "I told them not to worry about me. They'd have used whatever little piece of information I gave them to hunt me down."

Dennis took a step toward her, but Ian moved between the siblings, as if unsure who might strike the next blow. "Enough," he barked. "I doubt that—" he stumbled a second time over the unfamiliar name "—that Katherine would have taken such drastic measures unless she felt she had no other options."

She looked up at him in amazement. Was he taking her side?

Dennis shook his head and dabbed at his bloody lip again. "It's unforgivable. For all we knew, she'd been kidnapped or murdered. We might have never known what had happened to her."

Ian turned to her. Now it was her turn.

"I was going to call them," she said. "Soon. I needed to get a permanent job and, if I could, my own apartment. I've been using a friend's." Dennis opened his mouth as if to interrupt, but she faced him down and plunged on. "I had to prove I could survive on my own, make my own choices. Good choices."

Dennis shook his head. "You don't understand them. They were just protecting you."

"I'm twenty-two years old!" she shouted. "When are they going to start trusting me?"

"Well, you certainly haven't shown good sense by pulling this stunt!" Dennis snapped.

Ian held up a hand as tears filled Katherine's eyes. "Hold on there," he said. "You're not being fair to your sister. She obviously did what she felt she had to. Whether or not you agree with her methods, you should respect her desire for independence."

Katherine stared at Ian as a wave of gratefulness swept over her. Dennis was always so sure he was right. Just like her father. Her mother had learned to hold her own against the males in the family, but even Julie Fortune, in her own way, had controlled her daughter's life. Most recently, her efforts to match her up with sons of her well-to-do friends had become totally unbearable.

"Well," Katherine murmured, "at least now you know where I am, and that I'm safe. You can go home and tell everyone."

But she knew that wasn't how it would work. She could see from Dennis's expression that her big brother knew it, too.

"Sure," he said. "I'll go home without you. Then who's going to catch hell? And Dad will be on the next flight out here."

Ian stood up and looked at the two of them. She wished she knew how much he hated her at this moment. Although he seemed to be hiding it awfully well.

After a long silence, Ian scowled at the scuffed toes of his imported leather shoes. "May I make a suggestion?"

"I'm not leaving Savannah," Katherine said quickly.

"I haven't said you should."

"But—" Dennis began.

Ian lifted a hand that commanded silence. "Dennis, are you staying in town?"

"At the Hilton."

Ian nodded. "Crofthaven, my family's home, is temporarily vacant. My father is off campaigning for the Senate. Why don't you join me there. If she likes,

Katherine can come, too. It will give the two of you a quiet place to discuss family issues, and I can play referee. Maybe you'll come to some kind of understanding."

"We can do that at the hotel," Dennis said, "just the two of us."

"No," Katherine glared at him, "you'd just try to bully me again."

"Good grief," Dennis complained, "I was trying to get you to come with me to the car so we could talk."

"Right." She rolled her eyes at him. "Next thing I knew, we'd be crossing the Tennessee border."

"Now children. Bickering won't help." Ian smiled at her, and she was suddenly grateful that he was there, trying to lighten the mood.

She turned to her brother. "It's not that I don't ever want to see them, Den. It's just that I need a little time. To be me. Without their interfering. If you like, we can talk about it."

He looked unsure. "All right. I can go by the Hilton, check out and pick up my things. If you think it's not too late to show up unannounced at your folks' place."

"Not a problem. There are always plenty of guest rooms, all made up. I'd ask you to my place, but there's not as much space." Ian turned to her. "It's going to be hard, for a while, getting the name right."

She blushed. "I'm so sorry, Ian. I intended to tell you everything. But for a long time I worried that if you knew, you'd contact my parents."

He smiled. "I might have. I can only guess how concerned they've been."

She shrugged, but she couldn't deny he was right. "I know. And I feel awful about that part."

"I'll call them in the morning and tell them I've found you," Dennis said.

"No." She gave him a sharp look. "I'll call them and apologize. And tell them I'm staying right here."

Dennis shot a frustrated look at the ceiling. "You have no idea how Dad's going to blow up if I come home without you."

She felt a twinge of compassion for her brother. "Oh, yes, I do."

It wasn't that she didn't trust her brother to take her to Crofthaven. Katherine chose to drive with Ian because she wanted to speak with him in private.

"Thank you," she murmured as he drove out of the city toward the estate. In the dark, the live oak trees along the highway looked like hulking giants, their graceful limbs and shrouds of moss only showing as deeper patches of darkness against the night sky.

"For what?" he asked.

"Standing up for me and for my dream."

"I just thought of how I'd feel if my family tried to force me to do or be something I didn't want."

"You work at your family's business," she pointed out. "You don't resent having your life predestined?"

He kept his eyes on the road, hands firmly on the steering wheel. "I always wanted to run Danforth's, or at least have a big part in the future of the company. Even when I was a little kid, before we added the coffee shops to the import part of the business, I loved hanging out at the docks, watching them unload the beans."

"Really?" she mused.

"I would have been disappointed if I hadn't been allowed to participate. But I wasn't worried. It's a tradition that the eldest son take over the company when his father resigns.'' He slowed the car to take a turn, and checked his rearview mirror to make sure he hadn't lost Dennis, following behind in his rental car. ''But I didn't walk straight into the CEO's job.''

''No?'' She loved to hear him talk. He had a rich, mesmerizing voice.

''I had to go to college, get a business degree, then work my way up through the ranks. I love what I do.'' He looked at her, and she could see in the way his eyes gleamed with life that it was true.

''What about the rest of your life?'' she asked. ''When you're not working.''

''Not much time for hobbies.''

''That's not what I meant,'' she said gently. ''You once told me you wanted a family.''

''I do, with the right woman, when the time is right.''

He turned once more, this time into a long driveway of crushed oyster shells, and pointed ahead at an ornate wrought-iron gate inscribed with the familiar D&D emblem. ''This is it, Crofthaven.''

She had expected a big house. Something spacious—graciously Old South, or maybe Nouveau Plantation. Katherine wasn't prepared for the grandeur of the beautifully landscaped grounds, tastefully lit by electric lanterns and hidden floodlights, or for the house itself when it came into view.

The mansion was of the Georgian style, popular in Savannah as well. Tall white columns graced a lofty front portico. Although additions might have been built onto the back of the house to expand it, the original main house must have been over a hundred years old, perhaps had even survived the Civil War. She could

imagine dozens of beautiful, period-furnished rooms
inside—formal parlors, dining room, ballroom, a li-
brary and many private bedrooms on upper floors.
Even lit only by moonlight, the place took her breath
away.

"The staff will have retired to their quarters for the
night. But Cook usually leaves something good in the
refrigerator for unexpected guests," Ian said as he
stopped the car and Dennis pulled up behind them.

"I'm not very hungry," she said.

In fact her stomach was in a turmoil. Seeing her
brother and Ian locked in mortal combat earlier had
shaken her more than she'd realized at the time. She
longed for simple comfort food. Something warm and
soothing.

"Well, maybe a cup of hot chocolate?" she thought
out loud as Dennis joined them.

"Done," Ian said as he lifted from the car's trunk
her overnight case, hurriedly packed with toiletries and
a change of clothing. They'd stopped by her apartment
for a few things on their way.

"I'll be good until breakfast," Dennis assured him
as he trailed after them into the foyer of the grand
house.

Her brother looked around, eyes narrowed critically,
but she could tell he was impressed and a little taken
aback by the Southern opulence. The house they'd
grown up in, overlooking a vast desert, was roomy and
casually comfortable in the Southwestern style. Their
mother had decorated with an eye to preserving ele-
ments of her husband's Native American heritage. But
the rambling ranch-style home, even with its pricey,
modern fixtures and appliances, wasn't what anyone
would call an estate.

Ian led them up the stairs to a second floor and down a long hallway lined with closed doors. He passed by several then opened one on his left. "Dennis, I think you'll find this comfortable. There's a private bath off to the side, and the morning sun warms up the balcony outside the French doors. The desk has a phone and the line is Internet ready if you want to plug in and check your e-mail. I notice you have a laptop with you."

"This is very generous of you, Ian," Dennis said. "Most employers wouldn't go to such lengths." Katherine began to relax a little at her brother's slightly friendlier tone, although he did sound curious about her relationship to Ian. "I take it my sister—"

"Will have a proper room of her own directly across the hall from yours," Ian supplied quickly. "I'm the first door on the right after you came up the stairs, in case either of you need me."

Was it her imagination, or had he added that last bit for her benefit? She intentionally avoided his eyes even as she felt herself blush.

"Cook usually has coffee on and croissants or bagels available by six in the morning. I'll leave a note for her to arrange a full breakfast in the dining room by seven-thirty. But sleep in if you feel like it. I expect, after your sister-hunting adventures, you're pretty tired."

"It wasn't the hunting that knocked the wind out of my sails." Dennis touched his swollen lip.

Katherine wanted to say he'd deserved getting slugged but thought better of it and just gave him a good-night kiss on the cheek. After all, maybe her family couldn't help seeing themselves as her protectors. It was going to take some reeducating to convince them she didn't need someone looking over her shoulder every minute of every day.

She followed Ian across the hall. He said nothing, just opened the door to the room she was to stay in and turned on the light.

A gasp slipped between her lips. The bedroom was decorated in shades of pearl-white, buttery cream and ivory with textures ranging from sateen-smooth to rich, deeply woven brocades. The only touches of color were an occasional whisper of pink in bolsters on the bed, tiebacks for the draperies, and a collection of delicate crystal perfume bottles and atomizers on the dressing table. The effect was of sun-warmed ice. She loved it.

"Whose room is this?" she asked.

"It was to be the nursery," he said simply.

Her heart stopped. She just didn't know what to say. "Oh, Ian." It took her a moment to recover. "It doesn't look like a baby's room at all."

"No. You see, my wife and I were going to live at Crofthaven, since my father was away more often than at home. But after— After the miscarriage, I hired an interior decorator to come in and—" he gestured, as if erasing painful memories with one sweep of his hand "—just paint it all white, I told her. Get rid of the primary colors and zoo animals."

She went to him, took his hand and held it to her heart as she faced him. "I'm so sorry. You didn't have to bring me to this room. I can stay in another. Really."

"No," he said, "I wanted you to see it."

"Why?" She couldn't imagine.

"I guess...I guess I just wanted you to know how

hard it was to let go of the idea of being a father. I'm not sure."

She shook her head. "You're still a young man. You can marry again." Her throat closed behind the words. She didn't want to imagine Ian with anyone else. She took time to really study him. His features were so strong and fine—his children would be beautiful.

"As they say," he muttered, "it takes two to tango."

He started to turn away, but she reached out and held him there, his right fist enclosed in her two hands like the center of a flower within her petals. He looked down at her. "What are you trying to do to me, Katherine?"

"I'm not sure. I just want you to know you can trust me. I'm sorry I lied to get my job. I'm sorry I misled you about my family life." He tried to turn away, but she stepped into his new line of sight. "Please listen to me. I took my college roommate's name because she suggested it. She's working in Europe for a year, and said I could have her apartment and borrow her name just long enough to get away from my family and start a life of my own. It seemed the perfect arrangement at the time. I know now it was wrong of me not to contact them. But you see what happened when they found me."

"Your brother said he just wanted to talk to you. I doubt he'd have hauled you back to Arizona against your will."

She laughed. "You don't know the men in my family. Oh sure, the Fortunes love their wives, daughters and sisters, but being males, and even more naturally pigheaded than most—"

"I'm offended!"

"—they believe they're always right. They run their own lives and everyone else's by their rules."

It was the first smile she'd been able to coax out of him in far too long a time. "And some people say I'm a control freak."

"Well…" She widened her eyes at him in gentle accusation.

He laughed and lifted her comforting hands to his lips, and kissed each of her knuckles separately. "I don't drag my women home by the hair like a caveman." His smile melted away. "Maybe I'm just as bad, though. I did force a woman to keep a baby and talked her into marrying me. That wasn't right."

"I don't suppose it was," she said. "But that doesn't mean you're a bad man. And it doesn't mean it wasn't the right decision at the time."

He paused a moment, then stepped closer and wrapped his arms around her. She sensed the embrace was as much to console himself as to hold her for the sensual pleasure of it.

"The one thing I learned from that tragedy is that there's nothing more important than love and trust. There can't be one without the other."

"I agree," she said.

"If Lara and I had truly loved each other, we might have stayed together, tried again. But I spoiled everything by forcing her to make decisions about marriage and children before she was ready. I often wonder if she had a premonition, of sorts, that our baby wouldn't live. Maybe that was why she didn't at first want to keep it."

"You're probably reading far too much into her decision."

He let out a long breath. "Maybe. But now there's this thing happening between us, Katherine. And I—" He moved her away from him just enough to look down into her eyes "—I still believe trust is crucial to any good relationship. And I don't know that I can trust you."

His words scraped her very soul raw.

Katherine swallowed and blinked up at him, willing herself not to cry. "I'm not the sort of person who runs around telling lies and deceiving people. It's just that I ran out of ways of dealing with my family. I had to separate myself from them."

She watched his eyes for any sign of judgment or blame, but his expression was carefully neutral.

"So what's your next move?" he asked, brushing his lips absently against her temple. His touch sent delicious shivers through her.

"I promised Den I'd call them, and I will. Soon."

"You could always fly home just for a short visit, to reassure them you're still the daughter they know and love."

She shook her head. "No. Not yet. If I go back, I might not have the willpower to leave again. I have to finish what I came here to do—prove I can survive without a parachute supplied by the Fortune money and name."

He drew her back against his chest and stroked her hair. When she looked up, he kissed her with such tenderness, she felt herself drifting toward a place they'd been before. An exciting, wild, delicious place.

She hoped that he wouldn't leave her that night. He might stay in this beautiful room with her, and they'd make love all the night long.

But he grasped her upper arms and firmly set her back from him.

"Ian?" she whispered.

"No. We can't do it, Katherine, not with this between us." He touched the tip of her nose. "Not that it won't tear me apart to walk out of here, with you looking so damn—" he winced "—edible."

"But—"

His eyes hardened. "Accomplish what you need to do. I'll be around to help you but only if you ask."

"But what about us? You and me?"

He shook his head. "I can't get seriously involved with a woman who's just visiting my life while she discovers her own. The woman I'm looking for must be willing to become a Danforth and help me make a family."

She felt empty inside. Dead. She couldn't speak.

He continued gently. "I understand that's not what you're looking for, Katherine. It's what you're running from."

He gave her a pained look. Then he was going out the door, closing it behind him.

"But," she whispered, "I love you."

Nine

Ian pulled on shorts and a T-shirt, grateful when the morning sun rose to join him. Sleep had been nearly impossible. He'd agonized the night away in the room that had been his as a boy and was kept for his use whenever he visited the estate.

Another man, he told himself, wouldn't have walked out of Katherine's room last night. Another man would have said to hell with the future. If Katherine wanted him for short-term gratification, then why not?

But he suspected a fling with Katherine would inevitably become more than that, and he knew only too well how hurtful a relationship could become when the people involved didn't agree on the important things in life, like marriage, children and honesty.

Those were the deal breakers.

Still it had been three in the morning before he stopped contemplating a quick sprint down the hallway to her room. Four o'clock before he'd finally fallen into a short, troubled slumber.

By seven he was ready for a run, figured he'd beaten everyone else out of bed. But as he approached the kitchen intending to check out Florence's preparations for breakfast, he could hear laughter coming from the kitchen.

Curious, he pushed through the heavy oak door to find Katherine on the phone, a cup of coffee in her free hand. His father's cook, Florence, was shoving a plate with a toasted English muffin and mound of orange marmalade in front of her.

Katherine looked up when he came in but kept talking. "I know. I realize the disaster I've caused in the newspapers, and I'm sorry I worried you and Mom." When she looked up at him, she grimaced. *My father,* she mouthed, and suddenly she looked so very young his heart ached. Twenty-two. It seemed forever since he'd been that age.

"Do you want anything now, Ian?" Florence asked.

"Thank you, nothing for the moment. I'll be back for a big breakfast." If he couldn't satisfy one hunger, he'd work on another. Ian gave Katherine a thumbs-up for good luck.

Thirty minutes later, he was back from a two-mile jog along the shore. Sweating and famished, he snatched up the towel he'd left on a peg just inside the kitchen door and slung it around his neck.

"Now don't you come dripping yourself all over my clean kitchen floor," Florence said. "It's unsanitary with all this food out." She shooed him straight through the kitchen and into the hall. "Come back when you're cleaned up. Breakfast will be on the table."

"Yes, ma'am," he said, catching a brief glimpse of Katherine laughing at him as she continued murmuring responses into the phone.

Katherine waited until Ian returned before she started in on her own breakfast, even though her muffin would be cold. She had asked Florence to let them eat in the kitchen; it felt cozier here than in the immense formal dining room. Ian sat across from her at the long, wooden trestle table, his plate piled with fried eggs, grits golden with melted cheese, biscuits fresh out of the oven and thick slices of grilled ham.

"So, how'd it go with your folks?" he asked.

"I was on the phone for over an hour." She shook her head, sipping the orange juice she'd helped Florence squeeze only minutes before. "They passed the phone around. I had to talk to my brothers after I'd spoken with Mom and Dad, then with my grandparents. I've been scolded enough for a lifetime."

"They weren't glad you called?"

She crunched into her muffin then sipped her coffee. It was the way she liked it—strong, with real cream and two sugars. The marmalade tasted homemade, tart and just sweet enough.

"It's not that. They just think I'm an idiot for doing what I did." She sighed. "I guess it was pretty childish of me not to stay and work things out, but I got so tired of it all."

"Maybe now they'll realize you have a breaking point. They might ease up if you went back."

This was the second time he'd mentioned her going home, and her stomach clenched at his words.

"Do *you* want me to leave, Ian? Is that what you're saying?"

"What I want isn't the point. You need to find whatever makes you happy. Maybe you don't realize what that is yet."

"Maybe," she murmured.

It made her sad to think that Ian could so easily suggest her leaving. Wouldn't he miss her even a little? What had happened between them was special to her. Yet he seemed to be able to put their intimacy out of mind so easily.

"Morning all!"

Katherine looked up from her plate to see Dennis stride with irritating exuberance into the room. "You look well rested."

"Slept like a baby. Maybe because I hadn't gotten more than a wink or two in days."

"I know the feeling," Ian muttered.

Katherine shot him a questioning look, but he merely shook his head.

"Took a while, though, to get to sleep." Dennis seated himself at the table with them and poured coffee from a silver carafe. "Your other guest kept me up. Poor, confused woman. Who is she?"

"Other than you, Katherine and me, no one else was in the main part of the house last night," Ian said, shooting a sly glance toward Florence.

The woman seemed to be struggling to hide a smile.

"What?" Katherine asked.

"The young gentleman apparently was visited by our resident ghost." She placed a plate of crisp bacon on the table, and both men dove for it.

Katherine laughed. "No, really."

"Really," Ian said casually. "Although I'm surprised she appeared to Dennis, here in the house. To my knowledge all her other visits have been outside, on the grounds or on the road to Crofthaven.''

Dennis stared at him, then turned to his sister. "He's pulling my leg, right?''

"I don't know.'' She eyed Ian solemnly.

Ian grinned at her mysteriously, forked up a bite of egg then bit off the end of a thick slice of bacon. "Many properties in and around Savannah have ghosts.''

"Did she speak to you?'' Florence asked.

Dennis looked thoughtful but didn't stop eating. Katherine couldn't remember a time when anything had got in the way of a Fortune man's appetite. "Actually, she did say something about going farther? Or maybe it was, 'fetch father.' I couldn't quite get it.''

"That's her all right,'' Florence crowed. She finished putting the food on the table, untied her apron and came to join them for her own breakfast.

Katherine frowned. "Are you sure you weren't just dreaming?''

Dennis polished off his first cup of coffee and poured himself a second. "She came into my room twice. I thought she must be one of the maids, or Ian's sister.''

Katherine munched her muffin, feeling a little left out. "I've never seen a ghost before.''

"Stay in Savannah for long, and you get to feelin' you might trip over 'em they're so plentiful.'' Florence chuckled.

Dennis turned to Katherine. "Are you going to stick to your promise to call Mom and Dad?''

"Already did,'' Katherine assured him smugly. "I have witnesses.''

He looked surprised. "What did they say?''

"That I should come home immediately."

"Are you going to?"

"Not a chance." She sat back in her chair and sipped her coffee contentedly. "I like Savannah, ghosts and all. And I love working for Danforth's. Back home, I'll always be Mom and Dad's little girl. Here, I'm whatever I choose to be!"

"Here, you're poor," Dennis stated.

She made a face at him. "Only temporarily. I'll work hard, save my pennies, move up in the company as I gain experience."

Dennis laughed. "Watch out, Ian. She'll have your job!"

She held her breath, waiting for his reaction.

His gaze settled on her, a mixture of admiration and something she couldn't quite read. "I expect your sister can do anything she sets her mind to."

The next day Dennis spent sight-seeing and reported his discoveries to his sister and Ian that evening when they returned from the office.

Ian took them out for dinner in old Savannah. Elizabeth on 37th Street took Katherine's breath away. Standing on the front porch of the old mansion and looking out over its lush garden, she found it hard to remember she was in the middle of a thriving modern city.

Inside, the decor was perfectly Southern in the oldest, most gracious style. And the food was pure bliss. Both of the men ordered herb-encrusted, grilled steaks as thick as Katherine's fist. She had trouble choosing but finally decided on a rich seafood soup chock-full of shrimp, scallops and local fish.

As they were leaving the restaurant, Katherine felt

as though she was being watched, but when she looked up and down the tree-lined street, no one seemed to be paying particular attention to her.

Still she felt strangely uneasy. It was the way she'd felt when Jaime Hernandez had looked at her in Ian's office. She climbed into the front passenger seat of Ian's car. "Have you been contacted recently by the cartel?"

"Not since our meeting in my office," Ian said.

Dennis leaned forward from the rear seat. "What's this all about?"

Ian sighed. "The company has had some trouble with a group from Colombia that would like us to buy our coffee beans from them. We strongly suspect they're linked to organized crime. The FBI was called in after a bomb went off in our headquarters here."

Katherine winced. She'd hoped he wouldn't mention the explosion. It wasn't the sort of thing her brother or parents would find reassuring.

"And this is the place you've chosen to work?" Dennis asked Katherine.

"That all happened before I started working for Danforth's. Besides, everything's under control now," she assured him.

"So now I'm supposed to go back to Arizona and assure Dad and Mom that you're perfectly safe, happy as a lizard on a sunny rock?"

"Well, I am," she said, and it struck her that it was true. She was happier than she ever remembered being.

Only one thing was missing.

Ian.

And it seemed to her that her chances of winning his trust might have run out.

* * *

Katherine delivered Dennis to the airport late the next afternoon. She had dreaded this moment. Not because he was leaving, but because his departure would leave her alone with Ian, and she didn't know what to say to him.

She desperately wanted to ask him what he was thinking about them. *Was* there a them? He had given her little or no hope that they could ever be together in a way she found acceptable. Perhaps because she had been so outspoken about not wanting to get seriously involved, he'd decided there could be nothing at all between them.

His attitude totally irritated her. Couldn't he at least give her time to think about it? Did they have to be an all-or-nothing couple? Whatever happened to having fun, dating, getting to know each other…falling in love? Slowly. She had always assumed marriage was years away for her.

She drove around the city, reluctant to return to Crofthaven to pick up her overnight bag. Now that Dennis had left, Ian would expect her to return to her own apartment. Abraham would soon return from campaigning.

This might be her last chance to clear the air with Ian, but she had no idea what to say to him.

It was dark when she turned into the tree-lined avenue that led to Crofthaven. The oyster-shell driveway crunched beneath the tires of the little third-hand car she'd recently leased. Few lights were on in the house, but a faint golden glow came from the upstairs window she knew to be Ian's room. She parked and let herself in the front door.

None of the usual staff seemed to be around. With an aching heart, she silently closed the immense oak door behind her and climbed the stairs from the foyer, still unsure of the right words, still hoping for Ian's understanding.

Did she love him? Absolutely. Did he love her? He'd never said so. Without love and a partnership based on equal rights, she couldn't commit herself to a relationship. Even with this strong, brilliant and exciting man. If marriage was the bottom line for him, how could she surrender all she'd fought for, just to become another woman buried in a powerful family of males?

She must tell Ian this. She must make him understand.

She would also tell him how much he mattered to her, if she could only find the right words.

Her fingertips rested on the doorknob of his room for minutes that felt like an eternity, before she worked up the courage to turn it. Only at the last second did she realize how presumptuous it was of her not to knock. She tapped with her free hand as she cracked open the door to a place full of male smells. His body, his aftershave, the pungent waxy scent of shoe polish.

"Yes?" Ian's deep voice, thick and distant with preoccupation.

She slowly moved into his room. He was sitting at his desk, the green glass of the lamp shade glowing in an otherwise dark room. He was in a T-shirt and briefs but didn't seem flustered by her appearance in his room. His face was cast in a soft wash of light, and he glanced up briefly, then back to the papers resting on the embossed leather desk blotter.

"I don't want to disturb you," she began hesitantly, "but I think we should talk."

"You do?" He didn't even spare her a glance this time.

She cleared her throat, which suddenly felt scratchy and tight. "I owe you an immense apology."

"We've already settled that. You did what you had to do. Family relations can be complicated."

"There's more to it than that, Ian. When it all started, I didn't know you. I didn't think that pretending to be someone else would matter to someone who hired me for a few weeks. I mean, how could I know how I'd feel about you. About us."

"Us," he repeated, his voice as sharp as glass shards. "Katie, I—" He shook his head, finally standing up to face her. He looked strained, his eyes as sad as a disappointed child's. "We want different things. That won't change. To be honest, I see no future for us."

She very nearly cried out her denial. "But that's just it! Maybe we need to give ourselves a little more time to see if what we think we want is really what we do want." She bit down on her lower lip, determined not to lose all self-control. "That wasn't very eloquent, was it?"

"No," he said bitterly, "but I get the gist of it. You want to keep your options open."

It sounded so shallow, the way he put it.

She drew a shuddering breath for strength. "Ian, I want to be careful not to make the wrong decision. Can't we please take things slowly and see what happens?"

"No." He came around the desk and took her hands in his. "I'm past the age of experimentation, Katherine. I'm not interested in trial relationships. I'll date casually for business purposes, for relaxation, and to keep my family off my back. But dammit, I won't get emotionally shackled to a woman who doesn't know what the hell she wants!" He dropped her hands and stepped away from her. "Losing my heart isn't an option for me."

"Well, it wasn't with me, either," she whispered, tears finally winning the battle. "But I have—"

He frowned at her as she struggled to keep her chin high. His voice suddenly turned gentle. "Katherine, don't say things you don't mean."

"I do mean it. Unfortunately," she sniffled. "Guess I didn't realize it at first. I never intended to care for you like this. I didn't want the man I someday fell in love with to be like you."

"Thanks a bunch," he grumbled.

"Listen to me!" she cried out in frustration. "You're what I've been running from!"

"This just gets better and better." But a wry smile tipped up the corners of his lips.

He was making fun of her, yes, but this was better than his sullen mood moments earlier.

She spoke quickly, as clearly as she could despite the tears. "The thing is, you come from money. When someone close to you is in trouble, you step in like some kind of superhero and try to fix it."

"And this is bad?"

She punched him halfheartedly in the chest. "Well yeah, if you never let people deal with life on their own."

Ian caught her fist between two hands before she could withdraw it. "And you're saying I've done that to you?"

"Not yet," she admitted. "But it's there…inside of

you." She tapped his chest with their linked hands. "If we stayed together, it would happen, in time."

"Maybe, since I've been made aware of your need for independence, I'd make an effort not to bully you."

She studied his eyes, so serious. Could she trust him with her life? With her entire future? "Is it even possible, Ian? I mean, you said with Lara, you forced her to do what you wanted. Is it possible for a person to change?"

"Maybe it's not so much changing as learning. Every relationship is different, Katherine. We've been tiptoeing around ours, trying to figure out if there's a chance it could work for us. As soon as I indicate that I want a family, you give me one of those terrified looks. As soon as you start running, I back off."

"It's true," she admitted sadly.

"We have to call a truce." He was holding her now, stroking her back softly, speaking into the wisps of hair at her cheek. "We have to stop reacting to our fears, if we're going to figure out what we really want."

Back in Arizona, she'd thought she knew what she wanted—freedom to do whatever she chose. But with freedom came responsibilities, and complications she hadn't foreseen.

"I like working for Danforth's, even if it means hard work and not making a lot of money. But my loyalty to the company got all tangled up with my loyalty to you, Ian."

"Maybe it's just an old-fashioned crush on the boss?"

She shook her head vehemently. "It's more than that. I like being close to you, and I respect what you're trying to do. Protecting your employees, your father and family. I want to be part of what you are and what you do. I just haven't figured out how." That was as clear as she could make her thoughts for the time being.

He nodded, as if willing to accept this much on faith.

"What about you, Ian?" she asked, her voice sounding thin and unsure to her own ears. If he told her to go away now, after she'd poured her heart out to him, she'd have to leave Savannah. It would break her heart to see him in the offices or around the city, and not be able to be with him.

"Heaven help me, but I've wanted you, Katherine, from the moment you walked into my office." He kissed her then, tenderly but thoroughly. He kissed her as if he'd been thinking about doing it for a very long time. But when he drew back and he looked at her, she could see that he still wasn't sure of her. Of them.

"If it was just the sex, it would be easy," he said. "I can have that with other women, but I don't care about them the way I do you. I want children, a wife I can love and who will love and nurture our children. And a home life that's good and healthy. And after the children are tucked in bed, I want passion. I want it all, Katherine. But if you can't promise me you'll be there for the whole show, I won't risk courting you."

Her throat ached with longing at his words. Ripples of need crested within her.

Could she be this person he envisioned? What would she do in Lara's place? What would she decide if she got pregnant?

The question came at her suddenly, demanding an answer. Demanding the truth.

She reached into her soul. "If I became pregnant...I'd love my baby. Our baby." She felt warmed from inside at the admission from her heart.

He studied her face, still cautious. "I'm not interested in being a single parent. Or a dad who visits on weekends. It's all or nothing with me, Katherine. I can't be any plainer."

"I understand," she said. But he still hadn't actually said he loved her. However, what they'd said this night was a start, a sharing of dreams, of ideals. "My mother says that all love is a risk."

"Some love is more so than others," he said.

She gazed up at him. "From where I stand, I think you're worth the risk."

He seemed to shudder from within, then his eyes darkened with a desire that she felt as physical vibrations between them. Tremors of passion, invisible but no less potent than an earthquake. "And you're worth the gamble, my darling," he said throatily. "But I'm going to have to do a few things to protect our mutual declaration of trust."

"Hire a bodyguard?" she asked, grinning as she wriggled suggestively in his arms.

"Not on your life. You can do anything you like with my body."

"Oh, I can, can I?" She ran a finger down the center of his T-shirted chest. Lower down, his briefs revealed a sudden tightness of fit.

"Mmm-hmm. Do with me as you will. As long as you leave me in one piece when you're done."

"I promise."

"And breathing."

"That, too?" She pretended to pout.

With a lusty growl he swept her off her feet, carried her three steps south and plopped her down on the bed. "To hell with breathing!"

She laughed, but only until his mouth covered hers, hot, demanding her full attention. She closed her long fingers around the back of his neck and head, pulling him still closer to deepen their kiss. His hands roamed her body, slipping beneath clothing, caressing responsive flesh, discarding whatever apparel stood in his way.

Her hands were no less busy, moving up under his T-shirt to tangle her fingers among the luxuriant, coarse hairs across his chest, rubbing her palms over his nipples until they tightened to hard masculine nubs. She slid her hand behind him to knead taut muscles the length of his back, down to his narrow waist, then pressed beneath the elastic top of his briefs to mold his male bottom.

She moaned with pleasure as his mouth caressed her breast. Liquid heat rushed through her as he alternately teased and sucked, lips and tongue driving her nearly insane with pleasure.

"I...oh, Ian! Please!"

"What?"

"Now. In me!" She gasped, barely able to breathe, opening herself to him, curling her fingers into his rock-hard shoulders now gleaming with sweat.

"You're the boss."

The seconds it took him to provide protection seemed far too long. She couldn't bear to lose touch with him. She cupped him from beneath, delighting in the weight of his sex in her palms as he slid the smooth latex over his erection.

He pressed her back down on the bed, wedging apart her thighs with his knee. As if he knew she had been ready since the first moment he touched her, he slid hard and fast and fully into her. She let out a cry of intense satisfaction, glorying in his size. She arched her back and lifted her legs up around his hips, encouraging him deeper still.

He thrust, and thrust, and thrust again…until she felt crazed with the heat and the wetness. She clung to him, wrapping herself around him as his deliciously slick, male rigidity pressed into her again and again. Coaxing from her eager body wave after wave of delicious, satisfying pleasure. She blazed. She sparkled.

Then the world blew away, leaving only this man and this moment, and nothing else at all.

Ten

Pleasures given and taken. Physical and emotional highs soaring ever higher. That was how the night passed. Just when Katherine thought her body had spent every ounce of its desire, when she had given all that she could, Ian came to her again, demanding more of her and of himself, pleasuring her beyond imagination.

When daylight finally coaxed Katherine from her dreamless slumber, she turned, naked in the twisted sheets, and looked across the pillow, expecting Ian to be there.

A note rested on his pillow beside a single red tea rose, undoubtedly clipped from Crofthaven's garden.

Urgent business. Leaving you with immense reluctance. See you tonight? Ian.

Katherine smiled drowsily, turned over and drifted back to sleep.

That night, Saturday, and the next day, Ian spent at Katie O'Brien's borrowed apartment. They spoke openly of their families, their dreams, their needs.

They made love.

Katherine had never been happier, and Ian smiled more than she or, she suspected, anyone else had ever seen him smile.

When Monday came, he told her, "Stay home, rest."

"But I have to be at the office," she objected.

"There will be nothing for you to do today. I have meetings all morning and most of the afternoon. I'll transfer my calls to the cell."

"You're sure?" she asked. She admitted to herself that she was exhausted. Where did the man get his stamina? He was amazing!

"I'm sure." He gave her a look she couldn't interpret. "Stay home. Tonight, we'll talk more."

"All right," she agreed, and kissed him goodbye, only too happy to snuggle in bed for a few more hours.

There would even be time to tidy up the apartment and do some serious window-shopping along River Street, she thought dreamily.

Holly looked up from her desk and frowned as Ian walked into her office. "You're sure you want to do this?"

"I'm sure," he said.

"She'll be very disappointed. Katie told me she really wants to stay with Danforth's."

"I know, but I'll explain everything to her tonight. She'll understand why I need to do this."

"Tonight?" Holly lifted a neatly waxed brow in surprise.

"None of your business," he snapped good-naturedly, then laughed. "Not yet anyway."

Everything would be put straight in good time. His personal and work life had always been kept separate, because that was how he liked it. Katherine had said she understood this.

Of course, that was just after they'd made love, when she'd lain in his arms, as mellow as a daisy in the summer sun. He wasn't sure how closely she was following his words as she nodded in happy compliance.

He leaned over Holly's desk to sign the papers faxed, at his request, from the temp agency.

"So, let me get this straight," Holly said as she gathered them up into a neat stack. "You don't want me to inform Katie that you've asked for her removal."

"Right."

"And when she comes in this morning—"

"She won't be in today." He chucked her pen into the ceramic jar on her desk, feeling in full control now that this detail had been resolved to his satisfaction. "Don't worry, she'll be fine with this."

She shook her head as she stapled the sheets together. "If you say so."

Ian arrived at the apartment armed with champagne and roses. As the day progressed, he had begun to worry, mildly, about telling Katherine what he'd done. But he reassured himself that his plans for their future were what she wanted, too.

Since she needed to feel she was making important decisions, too, and he understood that a woman's engagement ring was important to her, he hadn't yet bought a ring. He would take her to the best jewelry store in Savannah tomorrow, let her choose anything she liked. As big a diamond as a goddamn apple! Fine with him.

He found her apartment door ajar, as if she'd seen him through the window and unlocked it for him. As soon as he walked in, the aromas of frying onions, sizzling beef, and a heady blend of spices struck him.

"And she can cook, too?" he called out.

Katherine peeked around the corner from the kitchen into the living room. "Authentic Southwestern chili, with homemade tortillas."

"I've died and gone to heaven," he groaned. "Does champagne go with Mexican?"

"Champagne goes with anything!" She freed the bottle from his left hand.

He brought the roses out from behind his back with a flourish.

She gasped. "Oh, my!" Her eyes sparkled as she cradled their tissue-wrapped blooms and breathed in their scent. "If this is what Tex-Mex earns, what will filet mignon produce?"

"Chocolate…for dipping."

"What do we dip?"

"For starters, how about you?" He shot her a wicked grin.

She laughed. "Sounds like I'll have to be careful of what I cook when we have company."

He glanced toward the kitchen. "What can I do to help?"

"Set the table?"

"I can do that," he said, and pitched right in.

Katherine placed a steaming bowl of chili in the center of the little kitchen table, beside a vase for the roses. Next came a salad of mixed field greens drizzled with olive oil and balsamic vinegar. Warm tortillas were stacked on a platter beneath a damp cloth to keep them from drying out too fast.

They sat side by side, rather than across the table from each other, and Ian felt as close to her as he had felt in her bed. Two people, sharing food, sharing their bodies. Life was good.

Ian helped himself to a plateful of food and dove in with relish. "I don't think I've ever tasted chili better than this." He sighed.

"An old family recipe."

"Really?"

"My dad and uncles are chili fanatics. They also roast a mean pig."

"Sounds like your family eats well."

Her eyes took on a distant look. "We…they do."

"You miss them?" he asked.

She gave this some thought, and he watched as a series of emotions played across her soft features. "I didn't think I would, but I do."

"Why don't you take a week or two and go visit?"

"I don't know. Won't you need me at the office?"

It was the opening he'd been hoping for. He laid down his fork and leaned back in his chair. "Actually, I wanted to speak to you about that."

"The office?"

"Yes." He rushed on, wanting to get to the best part. "You see, I stopped by Personnel today and arranged for the temp agency to withdraw you." Her expression tightened, but he smiled reassuringly. "It's necessary, darling. There's no way we can work together. Even before I slept with you, just seeing you reduced my gray matter to sludge."

"But we make a great team!" Her cheeks flushed nearly as bright as her roses. "You said so yourself, after the gala."

He held up a hand, and her eyes snapped to it as if he was raising it in threat. "You don't understand," he said quickly, worried because the conversation seemed to be slipping away from him.

"I do understand." Her voice crackled with emotion. "You've pulled rank. Made a totally unilateral decision."

He opened his mouth to object, but she raced on.

"You have completely disregarded my feelings. There's no written law that bans me from your office or working for Danforth's in any way, just because we're having an affair!"

"An affair?" He nearly choked on the words. "Is that what you think this is?" He couldn't have been more shocked or hurt.

"We're two single, consenting adults who are having sex. What do you call it?"

"It's not like that at all," he said miserably. If she didn't understand the commitment he was about to make to her... Suddenly the words he'd thought would come so easily wouldn't come at all.

"What is it like, Ian?" Green eyes flashed defiance. "I'm allowed in your bed but not in your place of work? Is that what you meant the other night about keeping your personal and work life separate?" She stood up from the table, backing away from him when he reached out for her. "I just don't get it. I thought we were on the same wavelength this weekend. Have you been planning all along to push me out of the job I love?"

She was close to tears, he could tell, but fighting them.

He shoved back his chair and started toward her, but she was already backpedaling, brushing him away.

"If being your girlfriend is going to cost me my freedom to choose where I work and who I work for, maybe this whole thing is a mistake."

"I never said I wanted a *girlfriend!*" he ground out, seizing her by the arms, giving her a good hard shake to make her listen. "Or an affair." What he wanted was a wife, a woman to love forsaking all others, like in the vows they'd take. He wanted forever.

He had wanted Katherine Fortune. And no one less would do.

Tears came in a flood to her fiery emerald eyes. He was desperate to explain.

Dammit! Why hadn't he bought a ring? He could have whipped it out of his pocket. Dazzled her. Made his feelings clear to her.

But now he wasn't even sure he wanted to see his ring on her finger. He didn't like being told he was wrong. Liked even less being scolded.

Ian withdrew his hands from her arms and stepped back, glaring down at her. "Maybe this is for the best," he muttered thickly.

Katherine stiffened. "I suppose so." She drew a deep, shuddering breath and stared at the floor, as if it were a thin sheet of ice and she was surprised it was still holding her weight. "You'd better leave," she whispered.

He concentrated on containing his anger. *I wanted us to be married,* he thought. *I wanted you to have my babies.*

But he wouldn't say those words. Not to a woman

who was so centered on her own needs that she couldn't give him ten minutes to explain why he'd needed to do what he'd done.

Ian turned and walked out.

Staying away from Ian and the Danforth Building was the most difficult thing Katherine had ever done.

Somehow she found the inner strength to not pick up the phone and call him. She reminded herself, again and again, that she had every right to be furious with the man.

Hadn't she made it clear that she wouldn't put herself in another situation like the one she'd just run away from—a male-dominated, family-dictated life?

If she had toyed with the possibility of going home to visit, now she dismissed it out of hand. All she'd be doing was throwing herself back into the role of her parents' daughter at a time when she was most vulnerable. Once back in their house she'd succumb to the wish to be comforted. If she couldn't stand on her own now, she never would.

She called Holly just to make sure what Ian had said was true.

"I'm so sorry, Katie. I really am. I thought you were doing a great job. Everyone here will miss you."

"I'll miss them, too. Everyone except Ian Danforth."

Holly hesitated. "If I'm not asking too personal a question, what did you do to make him turn on you like that?"

I loved him, she thought sadly. "Dunno," she said.

"It's just not like him," Holly mused, sounding troubled. "He's not an easy boss, but he's always been fair."

"There's a first time for everything," Katherine said.

She thanked Holly for her help, and assured her she'd be fine. Then she called Execu-Temps and got herself a new job.

Katherine accepted a job working for a bank in the stockholder's department, typing correspondence and answering the phone. It was easier than working for Ian, but a lot less fun.

Two weeks later, she had straightened out her identity with the temp agency and moved on to a clerical position with an insurance company. After three days they asked her if she was looking for something permanent. Sure, she said.

Ian didn't call her or come to her apartment.

She was glad, she told herself. Absolutely thrilled to be rid of a controlling, arrogant, bossy...

Oh, hell, she thought, who are you kidding?

She'd loved him. Still loved him. But there was a difference between loving a person who was good for you, she told herself, and loving a person who was not. She would just have to be strong and get over him. Somehow.

Ian looked the FBI agent in the eye and asked, "Are you sure it was her?"

"Yes, sir." The man leaned forward in the chair opposite him. The agent had shown up late that afternoon with troubling news about the cartel's activities. "They've been keeping a low profile, but two of their men have been following the woman who was your assistant. Katherine Fortune, is it?"

"Yes." Katherine. It hurt just to hear her name

again. "You're sure they're connected with the cartel? Her family has been after her to come home, but I thought that was all settled."

"We don't make mistakes like that," the agent said dryly, then cleared his throat. "I guess you fired her? Mind telling me why?"

"I didn't fire her, I just asked for a replacement for personal reasons."

The agent nodded. "Personal reasons." He wrote something in his notebook. "It's possible the cartel believes she's still connected with you in some way. Perhaps these personal reasons?"

There was no doubt in his mind what the man was implying. "There might have been a time," Ian said. "But there's nothing between us now."

"I see." The agent nodded. "But the question is, do they know that? It's our theory the cartel might try to use someone in or close to your family to get to you."

Terror sliced, razor sharp, through Ian. "You think she's in imminent danger?"

"We'd rather be cautious at this point. Is there any way you might influence her to leave town for a while? Go somewhere she might be safe?"

Ian raked his fingers through his hair. There wasn't a chance he could talk Katherine into doing anything now, he thought grimly. She probably wouldn't even take a call from him.

Even if he called Dennis, and her family contacted her, she might refuse to leave Savannah on the grounds they were bossing her around again.

Stubborn, stubborn woman.

Her green eyes and sweet face appeared before him. His heart soared, then just as quickly, plummeted.

He'd lost her through his own fault. Worse yet, no matter how many times he'd told himself that he was over her, he wasn't.

"Mr. Danforth?" the agent said. "Can you help us out here?"

Ian looked up out of his misery, and in that moment a solution for at least one problem came to him. "I think I have a plan."

Katherine walked down the street, past the Danforth Building, making a point of not looking at its gracious facade or the distinctive D&D insignia she'd so often admired, scrolled across the doors. The time she'd worked behind those doors had been the most exciting weeks of her life.

But she wouldn't think about that now. It was over. The job. Ian. It was all over.

The spring morning was gorgeous, and she wouldn't let mooning over a man spoil it for her. She'd left early for work so the sidewalks weren't at all crowded. She enjoyed feeling as if the city was hers alone.

She crossed Congress Street, checked out a wonderfully jaunty hat in a display window. But as soon as she started to walk again, she sensed a car moving slowly along the street as if it was pacing her. She intentionally stopped and turned to look in a jewelry-store window, hoping the vehicle would keep on going. All the talk about cartels and bombs in weeks past was evidently playing tricks with her imagination.

The sapphire bracelet resting on a white velvet cushion was lovely, but her nerves suddenly pricked at the sound of a car door opening. Reflected in the plate glass, a tall figure came up behind her.

She bolted. Strong fingers wrapped around her arm. "Come with me," a deep voice said. "Now."

With a gasp, she spun around, ready to scream. But the cry died in her throat and all that came out was a whimper of surprise and irritation at the sight of Ian.

Katherine glared at him. "You scared me half to death." She tried to pull away, but he tightened his grip.

"You're in danger. I'm taking you someplace safe."

She laughed. "Don't be ridiculous. I have a job and I'm going there now. Let me go. And don't bother calling. I won't even listen to your messages."

"That's why we have to do this my way," he growled.

"You just don't listen, do you?" She tried jamming her fists down on her hips in a show of defiance, but he wouldn't let go of her arm. "Ian, manhandling a woman is no way to convince her to stay with him. I'm my own w—"

He pulled her roughly to him, kissed her firmly on the mouth then heaved her over one shoulder much as she imagined he would have a sack of coffee beans.

"Put me down!" she screamed.

The few people on the street stared at them, as though unsure what to do.

"Lover's quarrel," Ian mumbled cheerfully at a couple walking past. "She adores makeup sex."

The man laughed, but the woman didn't look reassured.

Ian dumped her into the driver's seat of his car and climbed in after, shoving her over with his hip. The car's engine was idling.

He hit the child safety lock before she could reach for the door latch. "Uh-uh," he cautioned, immediately pulling into traffic. "You don't want to throw yourself out the door of a moving vehicle. Only in movies do people get up and walk away."

Katherine pressed her back against the black leather seat, arms across her chest, and glowered at him. "I hate you."

"No, you don't."

"What do I have to do to prove that I don't want my life run by parents, brothers, a boyfriend or husband?"

"Have you considered the option of having no life at all?"

He was watching the traffic ahead. She couldn't see his eyes. "What are you talking about?"

"The FBI says you're being followed, and they're pretty sure your shadows are cartel thugs."

"Following me? Why? I have no influence over Danforth business policies."

"No, but they must think you and I—"

"Oh, please—"

"Shut up and listen to me," he ground out. "You saw the way Hernandez looked at you that day in my office. He figured you were my mistress."

She started to object, but he reached out and grasped her hand, gave it a warning squeeze. "These people are desperate, Katherine. They might try to use you to leverage me into a decision in their favor."

She went limp and slid down into the car seat as they sped out of the city. "So why didn't the FBI just warn me?" she asked, her throat suddenly hot and tight.

"Because, for now, that's all they could do. They don't have enough manpower to provide round-the-clock surveillance for everyone in my family, and you, as well. And I'm not convinced that just watching and waiting is the answer.''

She cast him a dubious glance. "So what is?"

"We're going to disappear for a while."

She could feel her anger swell again. But a voice from somewhere inside whispered that maybe, this once, his efforts to protect her might be justified. Even if kidnapping seemed a bit extreme.

"You said *we*. You're staying with me?"

He nodded.

"What about your work?"

"My laptop's in the trunk. All I need is a phone line to plug into. I'll retrieve my office e-mail and I can handle anything critical from a remote location."

"And my job?"

"Holly was able to track down your current employer. I've already called and left a message that you're sick and will be out for a few days."

"My family might worry."

"I have their blessing, per Dennis."

She sighed. "Sounds like you've thought of everything."

"I try." She could hear a note of satisfaction in his voice. The consummate manager.

Katherine couldn't help letting out a frustrated shriek.

"What?" he said.

"No matter what I do, I just can't seem to get my life running in a direction I want it to go."

He turned his head to look at her as he took an exit off the highway through a low-country glade. "A lot of people feel that way. Believe me, I don't want to take away your freedom, Katherine. I never wanted that. After this is over, if you never want to see me again, I'll respect your wishes. But I can't let them hurt you. It's because of me you've become a target.''

She looked deeply into his eyes and could see that he meant what he'd said. It wasn't power over her that he wanted. He was all about doing the honorable thing. He saw her, for the moment, as his responsibility. He cared what happened to her. It was that simple.

''All right,'' she said, finally letting down her defenses, ''so where are we disappearing to?''

Tybee Island wasn't far from the glamorous city of Savannah. But there were pockets of secluded marshland and cottages off the beaten track taken by locals and tourists headed for Tybee's popular beaches. It would be difficult to find a person who didn't wish to be found, even if someone knew that's where they were headed. Besides, the cartel was looking for someone named Katie O'Brien, and she was safely in London—making Ian and Katherine's job of disappearing that much easier.

The cabin, as Ian remembered it from a rare hunting excursion with his father, was a rustic, one-room affair, kept well-stocked with food and spare clothing on the chance one of the boys would drop in for a weekend of duck hunting. The key, Ian knew, would be under the porch.

Ian led Katherine down a grassy hillside to an inlet off the bay, patches of water glistening in the sun where cattails and sea grasses hadn't filled in. A canoe had been pulled up onto the shore—an invitation to explore this watery world. An elegant great blue heron stood, matchstick-thin legs deep in brackish water, stoically eyeing the rippling surface for signs of prey—a slow-swimming minnow, a careless frog.

Katherine froze, watching the immense bird, her expression absorbed.

Ian stepped closer to her. "Are you all right?"

"Better than all right," she murmured. "This is beautiful." She turned to face him. "You can kidnap me anytime."

He guessed she didn't mean anything by it, just a comment to break the last strands of tension between them. But something about the way she leaned a little closer to him tugged at his heartstrings, and he wrapped his arms around her and nuzzled her head. He was ready to release her the instant she objected. She didn't.

When she looked up at him, her eyes were brimming with emotion. He couldn't help himself. He kissed her deeply, long and hard.

"I've missed you," he whispered.

"Me, too." She shook her head then pressed her cheek to his chest. "I wish this were simpler."

"The complications over the cartel?"

"No, us."

His heart stopped, then kicked into high gear. Was there a chance? What was she trying to tell him? He swallowed, sensing that every word he spoke now was important. Desperately he searched for the right ones.

"Maybe we've made things more difficult than they need to be."

"You think?" Her eyes shone, liquid emeralds.

"Maybe." He kissed the bridge of her nose, her forehead, an auburn curl that toppled over it. "I'm sorry I've handled things so autocratically. I don't mean to do that—boss you around, make decisions for you. It's just that it's my father's way. As much as I hated him pulling rank while I was growing up, I suppose I've inherited some of his tactics. I never intended to hurt you, or rob you of your independence.''

She thought for a moment. ''I suppose that's the way it is in my family, too.''

''How's that?''

She shrugged, wrapping her arms around him to pull him even closer, although they were already chest to chest. ''The men see it as their duty to protect their women. And we women either succumb to the paternal order, or rebel. I'm one of those who had to rebel.''

He chuckled, giving her a squeeze. ''So I've discovered.''

Katherine turned her head to one side so that she wouldn't have to pull away to see his face. ''Ian?''

''Yes.''

''Is there still room for compromise?''

''With your family?''

''With us.''

He felt as if he'd been holding his breath for days. No, weeks. Knowing Katherine Fortune was like watching a movie, trying to guess the ending, and always being surprised no matter how many times you saw the film. She kept changing the last scene!

Perhaps every couple faced a moment in their relationship when an invisible line was drawn by fate. Words were said, mistakes made. Once you crossed over, you could never cross back. He had let her down in ways he hadn't understood but were vital to her.

But now…now he wondered about second chances.

Slowly he lifted her chin and gazed into her misty green eyes. ''I was terrified you'd never let me get close to you again.''

She smiled and, incongruously, tears spilled over. ''I was terrified I wouldn't have the strength to walk away from you, if you couldn't see clear to letting me be me.''

His heart leaped with new hope. She was opening a door for him. He lifted her fingertips to his lips. ''If you weren't you, I wouldn't love you.'' And he saw something wonderful light up in her eyes.

''Let's talk. Really talk,'' she whispered.

Eleven

The hard parts they handled out on the water. Gliding across the smooth surface of a cove, sheltered by tall cattails and ancient cypress, they paddled the canoe and emptied their souls. Out in the middle of the marsh it was impossible for either one of them to walk away in a heated moment.

Katherine knelt up front with her paddle, while Ian sat in the carved-out seat behind her with his. At first the coordination of paddling was as tricky as maneuvering through the pitfalls of their conversation. Sometimes she wanted to move the sleek yellow hull in one direction, and he paddled at a different angle, so that they ended up at a destination neither of them had intended.

And sometimes their discussions sank to the level

of frustrated paddle slapping on the water, resulting in wet clothing, tears, or pauses to hold each other, kiss and reassure.

They agreed on one rule. Silence wasn't an option. They must keep talking, keep on sharing whatever they felt or needed or believed in. After the third day of navigating through each other's emotional highs and lows, and the mazelike brine marsh, they discovered they agreed more often than disagreed.

And they made love whenever they liked, which was often. In the morning before a breakfast of French toast, maple syrup and spicy sausages. In the afternoon following hours of rowing, counting swans, geese and birds neither could identify. At night to the accompanying gentle hoots of owls.

Katherine and Ian made love. They healed. They became one.

On their fifth day in the Tybee Island cabin, Ian sat on the edge of their bed and retrieved messages from his office. When he shut off his cell phone and turned to face Katherine, he was smiling. ''The FBI picked up the two men who were shadowing you. They were illegal aliens from Colombia and are being deported.'' She gave an exultant shriek, and he took her in his arms and fell back against the pillows. ''It's safe to go home,'' he said.

Yet she wasn't sure she wanted to go back to Savannah. Why leave paradise? Except that the real world couldn't be put off forever. ''Back to my job at the bank,'' she murmured, and looked up at him.

"Unless you'd rather come back to Danforth's," he said.

"In a heartbeat!" she cried, then thought about all they'd discussed. "I agree with you, though, I'm not sure it's best that I continue working as your EA."

He looked relieved. "You're good with people."

"Yes." This was something she'd only recently learned, and it pleased her, this talent she hadn't known was hers.

"You like Holly?" he asked.

"I do, and she's been really nice to me."

"Think you could work with her?"

Katherine pushed herself up out of the nest of bedclothes to look at him. "You mean, in Personnel? She'd be my boss?"

"How do you feel about that?" It was a phrase he was learning to use more often in their conversations.

"I like it. I didn't know there was an opening."

"Holly left me an update on job openings. Of course, that doesn't mean you'd have to stay there forever. It's a good entry-level position that might prepare you for supervisory jobs, and eventually an executive position, if that's what you want."

She grinned. "I'll take it!"

"I'll call and tell Holly it's filled then."

"Speaking of filling…" she said, wiggling her bottom into an inviting portion of his anatomy.

He rolled his eyes dramatically. "My work is never done."

"Shut up and just—" *Kiss me,* she thought, as he covered her mouth with his. And in a moment he was right where she wanted him.

* * *

The next day they returned to Savannah. The car was packed by ten in the morning, and Katie closed the door of the little cabin with a reluctant sigh.

"Mixed feelings?" Ian asked.

"I'm looking forward to my new job, but I'll miss this little place."

"We can come back," he offered. "As often as you like." He seemed to hesitate. "There's one more thing I have to do before we leave." His expression was serious, and her nerves prickled in warning.

"Yes?"

Instead of responding, he reached into his pocket and pulled out a thin, round object, then he was down on one knee in the grass before her. Her heart stopped. Her mouth went dry.

"I know you said our difference in age doesn't matter," he began with endearing awkwardness. "And I know you're still a little worried about marriage, but if I promise I'll never stop you from doing anything your heart tells you to do, but stand by you when you need me…will you please marry me, Katherine Anne Fortune?"

She looked down at her finger as he slipped on the ring. She expected to see the flash of a diamond, even though a plain, unadorned band of gold would have been enough. She frowned at the ring, then at him.

"It's grass."

"No jewelry store in the glade." He looked sheepish, embarrassed, then worried. "I made it myself. I know you have strong feelings about a lot of things, and long ago I decided that when I asked you to marry me, I'd wait to let you choose your ring. This is to hold that place on your finger for me."

She touched the simple braid of reeds he'd fashioned for her and was deeply, profoundly touched. "I'm not sure anything else would be as wonderful as this," she said.

"If you can't say yes to me now—if you need more time to think... I know you said you loved me, but if..."

The man who had cut billion-dollar deals was a nervous wreck. She'd be sadistic to make him wait for an answer.

"I'm going to keep on asking, Katherine, until you're ready. I'll wait as long as you need—"

She quieted him with a kiss. "I love you. I want to be with you. I want to be your wife."

"You do?"

"I do...now, about the wedding."

"We'll keep it small," he said quickly, guessing she'd want it that way.

"With two families like the Fortunes and the Danforths? No way. Big church wedding. Enormous cake."

"Delicate white tiers," he said.

"Chocolate!" she countered.

"A string quartet."

"Full orchestra." She grinned.

"Whatever!" He stood up, sweeping her into his arms and spinning around and around with joy until she was dizzy and begged him to stop. "You said you wanted children. How about two?"

"No fewer than four, I think." She laughed at his

look of happy surprise. "Did I tell you twins run in my family?"

"I wouldn't be surprised at anything you tell me, Katherine dear. I have a feeling, you'll keep me guessing for a very long time."

Oh, she thought, this is going to be good. Very good indeed.

*   *   *   *   *

Watch for the next book in the
DYNASTIES: THE DANFORTHS *series,*
CHALLANGED BY THE SHEIKH
by Kristi Gold, available in
June from Silhouette Desire.

Silhouette®

Desire®

DYNASTIES : THE DANFORTHS

**A family of prominence…
tested by scandal, sustained by passion.**

CHALLENGED BY THE SHEIKH

(Silhouette Desire #1585)

by Kristi Gold

Imogene Danforth knew her way around a boardroom,
but not around a horse. Sheikh Raf Ibn Shakir offered
to teach Imogene everything she needed to know…
but his asking price was not what she expected!

Available June 2004 at your favorite retail outlet.

Gaining back trust is hard enough…but especially when you're being set up for murder!

USA TODAY bestselling author

MARY LYNN BAXTER

Divorce attorney Hallie Hunter can hardly keep her composure when Jackson Cole walks through her door, begging her to represent him in an ongoing murder investigation in which he's the prime suspect.

Never able to deny her ex-fiancé, Hallie is thrust toward a dangerous underworld as she helps him confront a devastating truth—and must decide for herself if she can ever live without him again.

WITHOUT YOU

"The attraction between the hero and heroine sparks fire from the first and keeps on burning hot throughout."
—*Publishers Weekly* on *Sultry*

Available in May 2004 wherever paperbacks are sold.

Visit us at www.MIRABooks.com

MMLB2051

eHARLEQUIN.com

The eHarlequin.com online community is *the* place to share opinions, thoughts and feelings!

- Joining the community is easy, fun and **FREE!**

- Connect with **other romance fans** on our message boards.

- Meet your **favorite authors** without leaving home!

- **Share opinions** on books, movies, celebrities…and *more!*

Here's what our members say:

"I love the friendly and helpful atmosphere filled with support and humor."
—Texanna (eHarlequin.com member)

"Is this the place for me, or what? There is nothing I love more than 'talking' books, especially with fellow readers who are reading the same ones I am."
—Jo Ann (eHarlequin.com member)

Join today by visiting
www.eHarlequin.com!

INTCOMM

If you enjoyed what you just read,
then we've got an offer you can't resist!

Take 2 bestselling love stories FREE!

Plus get a FREE surprise gift!

Clip this page and mail it to Silhouette Reader Service™

IN U.S.A.	IN CANADA
3010 Walden Ave.	P.O. Box 609
P.O. Box 1867	Fort Erie, Ontario
Buffalo, N.Y. 14240-1867	L2A 5X3

YES! Please send me 2 free Silhouette Desire® novels and my free surprise gift. After receiving them, if I don't wish to receive anymore, I can return the shipping statement marked cancel. If I don't cancel, I will receive 6 brand-new novels every month, before they're available in stores! In the U.S.A., bill me at the bargain price of $3.57 plus 25¢ shipping and handling per book and applicable sales tax, if any*. In Canada, bill me at the bargain price of $4.24 plus 25¢ shipping and handling per book and applicable taxes**. That's the complete price and a savings of at least 10% off the cover prices—what a great deal! I understand that accepting the 2 free books and gift places me under no obligation ever to buy any books. I can always return a shipment and cancel at any time. Even if I never buy another book from Silhouette, the 2 free books and gift are mine to keep forever.

225 SDN DNUP
326 SDN DNUQ

Name	(PLEASE PRINT)	
Address	Apt.#	
City	State/Prov.	Zip/Postal Code

* Terms and prices subject to change without notice. Sales tax applicable in N.Y.
** Canadian residents will be charged applicable provincial taxes and GST.
All orders subject to approval. Offer limited to one per household and not valid to current Silhouette Desire® subscribers.
® are registered trademarks of Harlequin Books S.A., used under license.

DES02   ©1998 Harlequin Enterprises Limited

presents

You're on his hit list.

Enjoy the next title in
Katherine Garbera's
King of Hearts miniseries:

MISTRESS MINDED
(Silhouette Desire #1587)

When a workaholic boss persuades his faithful
assistant to pretend to be his temporary
mistress, it's going to take the influence of
a matchmaking angel-in-training to bring
them together permanently!

*Available June 2004
at your favorite retail outlet.*

Visit Silhouette Books at www.eHarlequin.com   SDMM

COMING NEXT MONTH

#1585 CHALLENGED BY THE SHEIKH—Kristi Gold
Dynasties: The Danforths
Hotshot workaholic Imogene Danforth was up for a promotion, and only
her inability to ride a horse was standing in her way. Sheikh Raf Shakir
had vowed to train her on one of his prized Arabians…provided she stay
at his ranch. But what was Raf truly training Imogene to be: a wonderful
rider or his new bed partner?

#1586 THE BRIDE TAMER—Ann Major
Forced to rely on her wealthy in-laws, Vivian Escobar never dreamed
she'd meet a man as devastatingly sexy as Cash McRay—a man who was
set to marry her sister-in-law but who only had eyes for Vivian. Dare they
act on the passion between them? For their secret affair might very well
destroy a family.…

#1587 MISTRESS MINDED—Katherine Garbera
King of Hearts
With a lucrative contract on the line, powerful executive Adam Powell
offered his sweet assistant the deal of a lifetime—pretend to be his
mistress until the deal was sealed. Jayne Montrose was no fool; she knew
this was the perfect opportunity to finally get into Adam's bed…and into
his heart!

#1588 WILD IN THE MOONLIGHT—Jennifer Greene
The Scent of Lavender
She had a gift for making things grow…except when it came to
relationships. Then Cameron Lachlan walked onto Violet Campbell's
lavender farm and seduced her in the blink of an eye. Their passion
burned hot and fast, but could their blossoming romance overcome the
secret Violet kept?

#1589 HOLD ME TIGHT—Cait London
Heartbreakers
Desperate to hire the protective skills of Alexi Stepanov, Jessica Sterling
found herself offering him anything he wanted. She never imagined his
price would be so high, or that she would be so willing to give him
everything he demanded…and more.

#1590 HOT CONTACT—Susan Crosby
Behind Closed Doors
On forced leave from the job that was essentially his entire life, Detective
Joe Vicente was intrigued by P.I. Arianna Alvarado's request for his help.
He agreed to aid in her investigation, vowing not to become personally
involved. But Joe soon realized that Arianna was a temptation he might
not be able to resist.

SDCNM0504